The Death of Ivan Ilyich

AND

Confession

OTHER TRANSLATIONS BY PETER CARSON

Fathers and Sons by Ivan Turgenev

PLAYS:

Ivanov; The Seagull; Uncle Vanya; Three Sisters;

The Cherry Orchard by Anton Chekhov

LEO TOLSTOY

The Death of Ivan Ilyich

AND

Confession

TRANSLATED BY PETER CARSON

LIVERIGHT PUBLISHING CORPORATION
A Division of W. W. Norton & Company
New York • London

Printed in the United States of America
First Edition

Manufacturing by Courier Westford
Book design by Chris Welch
Production manager: Louise Mattarelliano

Library of Congress Cataloging-in-Publication Data

Tolstoy, Leo, graf, 1828–1910.
[Works. Selections. English. 2014]
The death of Ivan Ilyich and Confession / Leo Tolstoy ;
translated by Peter Carson.
pages ; cm
Includes bibliographical references.
ISBN 978-0-87140-426-8 (hardcover)
I. Carson, Peter, 1938–2013, translator.
II. Tolstoy, Leo, graf, 1828–1910. Smert' Ivana Il'icha. English.
III. Tolstoy, Leo, graf, 1828–1910. Ispoved'. English.
IV. Title. V. Title: Confession. VI. Title: Death of Ivan Ilyich.
PG3366.A13C37 2014
891.73'3—dc23

2013018533

Liveright Publishing Corporation
500 Fifth Avenue, New York, N.Y. 10110
www.wwnorton.com

W. W. Norton & Company Ltd.
Castle House, 75/76 Wells Street, London W1T 3QT

1 2 3 4 5 6 7 8 9 0

To my daughter Charlotte

CONTENTS

TOLSTOY AND HIS TRANSLATOR

by Mary Beard

Leo Tolstoy died from pneumonia, aged eighty-two, at the railway station of Astapovo, a remote Russian village, on November 7, 1910. He had left his family home on October 28, in the middle of the night, walking out on his wife of forty-eight years—the long-suffering and increasingly paranoid Sonya. "I am doing what old men of my age usually do: leaving worldly life to spend the last days of my life in solitude and quiet," he wrote in the uncomfortably chilly letter of explanation he left for her.

In fact, there were to be very few of those "last days." For whatever Tolstoy's plans for the future had been (and we can now only guess at them), they were soon interrupted when he was taken ill on board a train and forced to get out at Astapovo, where the stationmaster gave him the use of his house. And there was certainly very little solitude or quiet. His death became one of the first international media "events." It attracted to the little station not only hundreds of his admirers (and some watchful government spies) but also a Pathé News camera team, eager to catch the great man's final moments on film, and reporters from all over the world who wired often unreliable stories back to their editors. "Tolstoy is Better . . . The Count Is Very Weak, but the Doctors Say There Is No Immediate Danger," blazed a headline in the *New York Times* just a couple days before his death, when he was already drifting in and out of consciousness. One of the most haunting images caught on camera is of Sonya herself, peering in through the window of the room in which her sick husband lay. She had traveled to Astapovo as soon as she heard of his illness, but the friends caring for him did not allow her in until Tolstoy was on the very point of death.

This drama at the railway station unfolded more than thirty years after Tolstoy had written the novels for which he is now best known: *War and Peace*, completed in 1869, and *Anna Karenina*, completed in 1877. His popular celebrity in 1910 owed more to his political and ethical campaigning and his status as a visionary, reformer, moralist, and philosophical guru than to his talents as a writer of fiction. Vegetarian, pacifist, and enemy of private property, he was, over the last decades of his long life, a persistent critic of the Russian imperial regime (hence the government spies infiltrating the crowds at Astapovo) and of the Russian Orthodox Church.

He came to favor a primitive version of Christianity based entirely on the teachings of Jesus, rejecting the dogma of Orthodoxy (hence his excommunication by church authorities in 1901). And he was a vigorous supporter of the Russian poor. He had launched welfare programs, including soup kitchens and funded schools. In a gesture of solidarity with the underprivileged, he renounced his aristocratic title ("Count" Leo Tolstoy) and took to wearing the characteristic dress of the peasants—though neither contemporary photographs nor the comments of eyewitnesses suggest that he ever really looked the part of an authentic laborer.

It was perhaps fitting that his final days became so celebrated across the world because, throughout his life but particularly from the late 1870s on, death was another of Tolstoy's obsessions. He had firsthand experience of death and the dying that was unusual even for a man of his era. As an active-duty soldier in 1854–55 he had witnessed the slaughter of the Crimean War, and he vividly recalled both the agonizing death of his brother Dmitry from tuberculosis in 1856 and the appalling sight—and sound—of a man being guillotined in Paris in 1857 (it was partly this experience that made him a staunch opponent of the death penalty). Of his thirteen children with Sonya, no fewer than five had died before they were ten. But in his writing he went beyond the horrors of death to reflect on the big questions that the inevitability of death poses for our understanding of life itself: if we must die, what is the point of living? Some of his most memorable reflections on this theme are found in the novella *The Death of Ivan Ilyich* and in the autobiographical memoir *Confession*. Both were written after Tolstoy had completed *Anna Karenina*: the novella was begun in 1882 and finished in 1886; the memoir was completed in 1882, but fell afoul of the Russian censorship efforts and was circulated only unofficially until it was published (in Russian) in Geneva in 1884. They are both powerful reminders of just how impressive Tolstoy's writing was, even when he had turned his back on those grand Russian novels that have become his main claim to fame. And turn his back he most certainly had: "an abomination that no longer exists for me" was his description of *Anna Karenina* in the early 1880s.

The Death of Ivan Ilyich, as its title plainly suggests, tells the story of the final months of one man: an ordinary, reasonably prosperous and successful middle-aged Russian judge. An apparently trivial injury (he hurts his side in a fall from a chair while hanging curtains in his new apartment) quickly develops into something worse. Doctors offer all kinds of diagnoses, medicines, and guarded reassurance, but within weeks, Ivan Ilyich can see that he is a dying man, confronted with the agony, indignity, loneliness, and (in Tolstoy's uncompromising description) foul stench of his own demise. For most of his family and colleagues, his death is an inconvenience and an embarrassment; they were, as the living usually are, relieved not to be dying themselves but simultaneously aggrieved by the reminder of their own mortality that Ivan Ilyich's death gave them. It is only a young servant, Gerasim, with all of Tolstoy's favorite peasant virtues, who can look the processes of dying in the eye and care for his master with true humanity; he deals unashamedly with excrement and allows the dying man to lie in the one position in which he can find some comfort—with his legs raised, resting on Gerasim's shoulders.

Confession is in a very different style and genre of writing: it is a first-person account of Tolstoy's own spiritual journey, from his rejection of religion as a young man, through his rediscovery of the Orthodox church in middle age, to his final rejection of the myths and falsehoods of the established church (from the Trinity to the Eucharist) while embracing the simplest moral teachings of Jesus himself. It is often taken as testimony to Tolstoy's spiritual "crisis" after he had completed *Anna Karenina*, and as a crucial point in his turn from fiction to politics and philosophy. But it also confronts the fear and the inevitability of death. It is in *Confession* that Tolstoy tells of his experience watching an execution in Paris and discusses his own dilemmas about suicide. And he broaches some of the major questions of the relationship between life and death that underlie the story of Ivan Ilyich: as he sums it up at one point in the memoir, "Is there any meaning in my life that wouldn't be destroyed by the death that inevitably awaits me?"

It is important to remember that when Tolstoy wrote *The Death of Ivan Ilyich* and *Confession*, preoccupied with dying as both those works are, he was still only in his fifties; he was to live another twenty-five years. Human mortality was for him, in large part, a philosophical dilemma. He also (as we see in *The Death of Ivan Ilyich*) relished the writer's challenge of intimately exploring the processes of dying—when it was something he could only have observed from the perspective of the living. It was a challenge that so intrigued him that he is later supposed to have asked his friends and followers to quiz him about the experience of his own death as he was going through it. "Did human perception of life change as one approached the end?" he wanted them to inquire. "Did one feel a progression toward something different?" Cannily foreseeing that, on his deathbed, he might be unable to voice a coherent response, he had even devised a code of eye movements to express his answers. But in their distress, those gathered around him in his final hours at Astapovo apparently forgot to pose the questions.

It is a poignant irony that Tolstoy's translator, Peter Carson, was much closer to death and dying when he was working on *The Death of Ivan Ilyich* and *Confession* than Tolstoy himself was at the time he was first writing them.

CARSON WAS ONE of the finest translators there has ever been of nineteenth-century Russian literature: "I am not an expert. I merely have a good feel for it," he once observed with typical modesty. That "feel" came partly from his family background in a social and cultural world that was in some respects not so different from Tolstoy's own. His mother was Russian, Tatiana Petrovna Staheyeff, the daughter of an extremely wealthy commercial family. She was not of the grand order of nobility from which Tolstoy, title or no title, originated, but her family too had turned a good deal of its substantial riches to the kind of philanthropy (founding schools, for example) that was such a major part of Tolstoy's life's project. When she was little more than a girl, she fled the Revolution in 1917, first to China, where she met her part-French, part-Anglo-Irish husband, and later to England. There, soon widowed, she brought up her children—Peter Staheyeff Carson, who was born in London in 1938, and his sister, another Tatiana—almost singlehandedly in a polyglot household where Russian, French, and English were spoken more or less interchangeably. In fact, the use of French side-by-side with Russian, so characteristic of the idiom of the Russian elite and noticeable in these works of Tolstoy (*comme il faut*, *établissement*, and so on), was very close to the idiom of Carson's early home life.

That "feel" came also, however, from a precise attention to language that was encouraged by his classical training. As a boy Carson won a scholarship to Eton, where he specialized in Latin and Greek, and he later majored in classics at Trinity College, Cambridge. It was an academic background that made him particularly alert to the forms and technicalities of language and expression. He insisted, for example, that in translating this "late Tolstoy," one should not make the mistake of imposing on it a literary, stylish rhetoric, as so many translators have done. *The Death of Ivan Ilyich* and *Confession* were both written more simply, even awkwardly, than *War and Peace* or *Anna Karenina*, with even more frequent repetitions of the same or very similar words (in the novella, for example, the words "decorum," "decorous," and "indecorous" recur again and again). Carson aimed to capture that particular side of Tolstoy's writing, retaining the repetitions (even though the works might have read more fluently if, as he put it, he had taken "evasive action" and "smoothed things over"), and so far as possible he also retained Tolstoy's sometimes surprising sentence structure along with his original paragraphing. He wanted the reader in English to be able to see what Tolstoy had been doing in the Russian.

Carson's main professional career, from the 1960s to 2012, was in British publishing at Penguin Books, where he ended up as editor in chief, and later at Profile Books. He had an almost unrivalled sense of what made a distinguished and sellable book. It was he, for example, who spotted the quality of Zadie Smith's *White Teeth*, and he brought the work of many other authors, myself included, into the world. His own style was one of extraordinarily elegant understatement: if he tapped his fingers together and said "I don't *think* so," you knew your latest scheme was a complete no-hoper; if he twinkled and giggled a little and said of a manuscript, "It's really *rather good*," you would know you had something close to a bestseller on your hands. And his talent was based on an equally extraordinary capacity for quick and careful reading: three novels in an evening plus six new book manuscripts over a weekend were his normal regime. I suspect that his life in reading and editing gave him a sneaking sympathy for Sonya Tolstoy, who often spent her evenings copying, recopying, and tidying up Tolstoy's manuscripts until the early hours, in addition to acting as an agent with his publishers.

Carson's translations were largely the work of his spare time. He agreed to translate *The Death of Ivan Ilyich* and *Confession* in 2009, when he could not possibly have known how uncomfortably relevant their themes would become to his own life—and death. For only halfway through the translation it became clear, in early 2012, that his longstanding illness would not be curable—and that, most likely, he had only months to live. He nevertheless pushed on with the task, determined to complete what he had begun, working whenever he could, sometimes from bed as he became frailer. The final manuscript was delivered to the publisher by his wife on the day before he died in January 2013. We can hardly begin to imagine what it must have been like to translate the grim tale of Ivan Ilyich as one's own life slipped away, but almost certainly the unsettling energy of Carson's version has something to do with the circumstances in which it was written.

Carson himself was very committed to the unusual pairing within the same volume of *The Death of Ivan Ilyich* and *Confession*. The novella has long been a favorite among the later works of Tolstoy and has attracted a wide range of interpretations and explanations almost from the moment of its publication. The aggressive and unforgettable "realism" of the description of Ivan Ilyich's final illness has prompted some critics to hunt for a factual source for the story, and indeed it does seem fairly certain that Tolstoy was partly inspired by the death of a judge called Ivan Ilyich Mechnichov who worked in the town of Tula, near the Tolstoy country estate, and whose sufferings had been described to Tolstoy by the judge's brother. Other readers—undeterred by the fact that, whatever real-life models there may have been, the story is essentially fiction—have attempted to diagnose the illness from which Ivan Ilyich was suffering, even though the elusive uncertainty about the nature of his condition is part of the point of the tale. Was it cancer of the gall bladder? Or was it cancer of the pancreas? Questions like these, as well as the lessons they might (or might not) hold for the palliative care of the dying, have ensured *The Death of Ivan Ilyich*, alone of all Tolstoy's works, an unlikely foothold in modern medical journals and libraries.

Much more significant have been the many discussions of the philosophical and ethical issues the story raises, in particular what in the end—after all the agony and the terror—allows Ivan Ilyich to approach death with some degree of equanimity? Or, to put it in terms of Tolstoy's own vivid image of the process of dying, what enabled him to struggle through that black sack into which he felt he was being pushed and make his way through to the light on the other side?

Tolstoy seems to offer two reasons. First, Ivan Ilyich finally came to recognize the failings of his apparently successful former life: among other things, its tawdry bourgeois aspirations, its vanity (it was, after all, a fall while hanging some curtains that led to his death), and the emptiness of his marriage.

> "Yes, everything was wrong," he said to himself, "but it doesn't matter. I can, I can do what is right. But what is right?" he asked himself, and at once fell silent.

This recognition of his errors is signaled in the narrative by two rare signs of genuine human interaction between Ivan Ilyich and his family: his wife at his bedside is caught weeping; and his young son, accidentally hit by one of Ivan Ilyich's flailing arms, takes his father's hand in his own and presses it to his lips, also in tears.

Second, at the very end of the story, Tolstoy insists that instead of attempting to avoid his own mortality, Ivan Ilyich at last managed to look death in the eye, and that direct confrontation destroyed the terrible fear which had until then so tormented him.

> He searched for his old habitual fear of death and didn't find it. Where was death? What death? There was no fear, because there was no death.
>
> Instead of death there was light.
>
> "So that's it!" he suddenly said aloud. "Such joy!"

Unlike *The Death of Ivan Ilyich*, *Confession* has had an insecure and fluctuating reputation since it was completed in 1882. In addition to the problems with Russian censors because of its attacks on the Orthodox church, Tolstoy himself changed his mind about the role and status of the memoir. It was first intended to act as an introduction to another of his religious essays, *An Investigation of Dogmatic Theology*, and originally carried the title *An Introduction to an Unpublished Work*. It was only when the first regular edition was published outside Russia in 1884 that it was entitled *Confession*. And it *is* simply *Confession*, not "*The Confession*" or "*A Confession*"; as Carson was keen to emphasize, this essay is not some admission of wrongdoing ("confession" in the usual modern sense), but an account of a spiritual journey in the tradition of the *Confessions* of Augustine or Jean-Jacques Rousseau. As such, in the late nineteenth century, it attracted considerable attention; in fact, it was one of the first of Tolstoy's works to be translated into English (before *War and Peace* or *Anna Karenina*). But it has often seemed less appealing to modern readers. It can seem self-indulgent in its introspection (the usual fault of spiritual autobiographies, however self-critical they set out to be); it includes some fairly austere discussion of philosophers from Socrates to Schopenhauer; and the idealization of the religious faith (and approach to death) of the Russian peasant, while touching, seems also naively romantic.

Confession comes to life again if we read it alongside *The Death of Ivan Ilyich* rather than alongside the religious essays with which it is usually grouped. The similarities and overlaps between the two instantly catch the eye: from the discussion of the inevitability of death to the nature of human self-deception and the admiration (romantic or not) of the honorable approach to life and mortality shown by Russian peasants (in contrast to the people, as Tolstoy puts it, "in our world"; that is, among the elite). In short, the pairing encourages us to see *The Death of Ivan Ilyich* as a fictional exploration of the theoretical problems of religion, morality, and mortality explored autobiographically in *Confession*. In other words, that question directly posed in *Confession*—"Is there any meaning in my life that wouldn't be destroyed by the death that inevitably awaits me?"—is answered by the novella.

Yet if *Confession* helps to expose the theoretical aspects of *The Death of Ivan Ilyich*, then the reverse is also true: *The Death of Ivan Ilyich* helps to expose the fictional aspects of *Confession*. Critics have often taken *Confession* as a more or less transparent account of Tolstoy's spiritual development from his youth, and especially of the religious "crisis" he went through after finishing *Anna Karenina*—a crisis marked first by his turn to the Orthodox church, then by his emphatic rejection of the dogma and lies of established religion. There are certainly many overlaps between Tolstoy's claims in *Confession* and what we know of his life, and of his intellectual and religious dilemmas, from other accounts. His son Leo, for example, in his own memoir of Tolstoy's life, *The Truth about My Father* (written, it is true, explicitly to defend Sonya from the attacks on her after the old man's death), claims to recall the very moment when his father rejected the Orthodox rules on fasting: during what should have been a fast for a strict observer of such things, sitting at the dinner table with the rest of the family, who were enjoying a hearty meal, Tolstoy pushed away his "ascetic fare," turned to one of the children, and demanded what they were eating. "Ilia, my boy," he said, "pass me the cutlets!" His days of formal religious observance were over.

It should go without saying, however, that autobiography is never quite transparent, and that first-person spiritual memoirs are always partly constructions—retrospective and simplifying fictions imposed on the confusing stream of memories and on intellectual doubts and dilemmas. In *Confession* Tolstoy hints at the very fictionality of his own autobiography through a series of echoes with his novels. At one point, for example, he describes his own fantasies of suicide almost exactly as he described those of Levin in *Anna Karenina;* this is not only a hint that there might be something of the real Tolstoy in the fictonal Levin but also that there might be something of the fictional Levin in the autobiographical Tolstoy. And we find many other close doubles between *Confession* and *The Death of Ivan Ilyich*—from the description of a dying man's attitude toward his own at first insignificant symptoms of illness to the image of the return to childhood that is so powerful in both works. It is as if *Confession* reminds us of the constructed nature of its autobiographical subject by anticipating many of the fictional tropes of the novella. Tolstoy was a man who defined himself *in* and *by* writing, in an inextricable amalgam of fiction and fact.

The Death of Ivan Ilyich and *Confession* demand that readers reflect on what the inevitability of death means to us, and on how we shall face our own end. At Peter Carson's funeral, the very last lines of *Ivan Ilyich* were read out.

> "It is finished!" someone said above him.
>
> He heard these words and repeated them in his heart. "Death is finished," he said to himself. "It is no more."
>
> He breathed in, stopped halfway, stretched himself, and died.

Carson himself might not have entirely approved of parading this alignment of literature and life which, in his own dying, he was concerned to downplay. Indeed, just three days before he died, he wrote:

> It is strange that I was smitten by my illness when translating *Ivan Ilyich* and *Confession*, but to be honest I do not think it has affected anything and I have no thoughts on the matter.

In Carson we had a man who had no interest in publicity and would have hated the celebratory—almost narcissistic—display of dying that unfolded at Astrapovo station (Carson in fact died at home with his wife). But happily, in a sense, his "thoughts on the matter" *are* preserved for us, and will live on, in this fine translation.

The Death of Ivan Ilyich

I

DURING A BREAK IN THE HEARING OF THE MELVINSKY case, the members of the court and the prosecutor met in Ivan Yegorovich Shebek's room in the big law courts building and began talking about the famous Krasovsky case. Fyodor Vasilyevich became heated, contending that it didn't come under their jurisdiction; Ivan Yegorovich held his ground; while Pyotr Ivanovich, not having joined in the argument at the beginning, took no part in it and was looking through the *Gazette*, which had just been delivered.

"Gentlemen!" he said. "Ivan Ilyich has died."

"He hasn't!"

"Look, read this," he said to Fyodor Vasilyevich, handing him a fresh copy which still smelled of ink.

Within a black border was printed: "Praskovya Fyodorovna Golovina with deep sorrow informs family and friends of the passing of her beloved spouse Ivan Ilyich Golovin, member of the Court of Justice, which took place on the 4th of February of this year 1882. The funeral will be on Friday at 1 p.m."

Ivan Ilyich was a colleague of the gentlemen meeting there and they all liked him. He had been ill for several weeks; people were saying his illness was incurable. His position had been kept for him, but there had been conjectures that, in the event of his death, Alekseyev might be appointed to his position, and either Vinnikov or Shtabel to Alekseyev's. So on hearing of Ivan Ilyich's death the first thought of each of the gentlemen meeting in the room was of the significance the death might have for the transfer or promotion of the members themselves or their friends.

Now I will probably get Shtabel's or Vinnikov's position, thought Fyodor Vasilyevich. *It was promised to me long ago and this promotion means a raise of eight hundred rubles, plus a private office.*

Now I must ask about the transfer of my brother-in-law from Kaluga, thought Pyotr Ivanovich. *My wife will be very pleased. Now she won't be able to say that I've never done anything for her family.*

"I thought he wouldn't leave his bed," Pyotr Ivanovich said aloud. "Such a pity."

"What was actually wrong with him?"

"The doctors couldn't make a diagnosis. That is, they did,

but different ones. When I saw him the last time, I thought he would recover."

"And I didn't go and see him after the holidays. I kept meaning to."

"Did he have any money?"

"I think his wife had a very small income. But next to nothing."

"Yes, we'll have to go and see her. They lived a terribly long way off."

"That is, a long way from you. Everything's a long way from you."

"He just can't forgive me for living on the other side of the river," said Pyotr Ivanovich, smiling at Shebek. And they started talking about distances in the city,[1] and went back into the courtroom.

Apart from the thoughts the death brought each of them about the possible moves and changes at work that might follow, the actual fact of the death of a close acquaintance evoked, as always, in all who learned of it a complacent feeling that it was "he who had died, not I."

So—he's dead; but here I am still, each thought or felt. At this point his closer acquaintances, the so-called friends of Ivan Ilyich, involuntarily thought that they now needed to carry out the very tedious requirements of etiquette and go to the requiem service[2] and pay a visit of condolence to the widow.

Closest of all were Fyodor Vasilyevich and Pyotr Ivanovich.

Pyotr Ivanovich was a friend from law school and considered himself under an obligation to Ivan Ilyich.

Having given his wife over dinner the news of Ivan Ilyich's death and his thoughts about the possibility of his brother-in-law's transfer to their district, Pyotr Ivanovich didn't lie down to have a rest but put on a formal tailcoat and drove to Ivan Ilyich's.

At the entrance to Ivan Ilyich's apartment stood a carriage and two cabs. Downstairs in the hall by the coatrack, leaning against the wall, was the brocade-covered lid of the coffin with tassels and a gold braid that had been cleaned with powder. Two ladies in black were taking off their fur coats. One of them, Ivan Ilyich's sister, he knew; the other was an unknown lady. Pyotr Ivanovich's colleague Schwarz was coming downstairs and, seeing from the top step who had come in, he winked at him as if to say, "Ivan Ilyich has made a silly mess of things; you and I have done things differently."

Schwarz's face with his English side-whiskers and his whole thin figure in a tailcoat as usual had an elegant solemnity, and this solemnity, which was always at odds with Schwarz's playful character, was especially piquant here. So Pyotr Ivanovich thought.

Pyotr Ivanovich let the ladies go in front of him and slowly followed them up the stairs. Schwarz didn't come down but stayed at the top. Pyotr Ivanovich understood why: he obviously wanted to arrange where they should play *vint*[3] today. The ladies went up the stairs to the widow but Schwarz, with a serious set to his strong lips and a playful look, indicated by a twitch of his eyebrows that Pyotr

Ivanovich should go to the right, into the room where the corpse lay.

Pyotr Ivanovich went in, feeling, as is always the case, at a loss as to what he should do there. One thing he did know was that in these circumstances it never does any harm to cross oneself. He wasn't altogether sure whether one should also bow and so he chose a middle course: entering the room, he started to cross himself and made a kind of slight bow. Insofar as the movements of his head and hands would allow, he looked round the room at the same time. Two young men, probably nephews, one of them a gymnasium pupil, were crossing themselves as they left the room. An old woman stood motionless, and a lady with oddly arched eyebrows was saying something to her in a whisper. A church lector in a frock coat with a vigorous and decisive way to him was reading something out loudly with an expression that permitted no contradiction; the peasant manservant Gerasim, stepping lightly in front of Pyotr Ivanovich, scattered something on the ground. Seeing that, Pyotr Ivanovich at once sensed the faint smell of a decomposing body. On his last visit to Ivan Ilyich he had seen this peasant in the study; he carried out the duties of a sick-nurse, and Ivan Ilyich was especially fond of him. Pyotr Ivanovich kept crossing himself and bowing slightly in an intermediate direction between the coffin, the lector, and the icons on a table in the corner. Then, when he thought the movement of crossing himself with his hand had gone on for too long, he stopped and started to examine the dead man.

The dead man lay, as dead men always do, especially heavily, his stiffened limbs sunk in the padded lining of the coffin with his head bent back forever on the pillow, and, as always with dead men, his yellow waxen forehead sticking out, showing bald patches on his hollow temples, his nose protruding as if it pressed on his upper lip. He had greatly changed, had become even thinner since Pyotr Ivanovich had seen him, but like all dead men, his face was handsomer, above all more imposing than when he was alive. On his face was an expression that said what had to be done had been done, and done properly. This expression also held a reproach or reminder to the living. Pyotr Ivanovich found this reminder inappropriate—or at the least one not applying to himself. This gave Pyotr Ivanovich an unpleasant feeling, and so he hurriedly crossed himself once more and turned, too hurriedly he thought, and not in accordance with propriety, and went to the door. Schwarz was waiting for him in the next room, his legs wide apart and both hands playing behind his back with his top hat. One look at Schwarz's playful, neat, and elegant figure refreshed Pyotr Ivanovich. Pyotr Ivanovich felt that Schwarz stood above all this and didn't allow himself to give in to depressing thoughts. The very way he looked stated the following: the fact of Ivan Ilyich's requiem cannot serve as a sufficient reason to consider the order of the courts disrupted; in other words, nothing can stop us unsealing and shuffling a pack of cards this evening while the manservant puts out four fresh candles; in general there are no grounds for assuming that this fact can prevent us from spending a pleasant evening, even today. He said this in a whisper to Pyotr Ivanovich as he came in, proposing they meet for a game at Fyodor Vasilyevich's. But apparently Pyotr Ivanovich was not fated to play *vint* this evening. Praskovya Fyodorovna, a short, plump woman who broadened from the shoulders down in spite of all her efforts to achieve the opposite, was dressed all in black with her head covered in lace and with oddly arched eyebrows like the lady standing by the coffin. She came out of her rooms with the other ladies, and taking them to the door where the dead man lay, said:

"Now there'll be the requiem; do go in."

Schwarz stopped, making a vague bow—clearly neither accepting nor rejecting this proposal. Praskovya Fyodorovna, recognizing Pyotr Ivanovich, sighed, went right up to him, took him by the hand, and said:

"I know that you were a true friend of Ivan Ilyich . . ." and looked at him, waiting for an action on his part that corresponded to these words.

Pyotr Ivanovich knew that just as in that room one had had to cross oneself, so here one must press the hand, sigh, and say, "Believe me!" And that's what he did. And having done it he felt that the desired result had been obtained: he was moved and she was moved.

"Come while they haven't started in there; I need to talk to you," said the widow. "Give me your hand."

Pyotr Ivanovich gave his hand and they went off into the inner rooms, past Schwarz who winked sadly at Pyotr

Ivanovich. "There's your *vint* gone! Don't take it out on us; we'll find another partner. Maybe you can cut in once you've gotten free," said his playful look.

Pyotr Ivanovich sighed even more deeply and sadly, and Praskovya Fyodorovna gratefully pressed his hand. They went into her dimly lit drawing room hung with pink cretonne and sat down by a table, she on a sofa and Pyotr Ivanovich on a low pouf built on springs that awkwardly gave way as he sat down. (Praskovya Fyodorovna was going to warn him to sit on another chair but found such a warning inappropriate for the situation and changed her mind.) As he sat down on the pouf, Pyotr Ivanovich remembered how Ivan Ilyich had arranged this drawing room and consulted him about this very pink cretonne with green leaves. On her way to sit down on the sofa, as she passed the table (the whole drawing room was full of furniture and knickknacks), the widow caught the lace of her black mantilla on the carving of the table. Pyotr Ivanovich got up to unhook her, and the sprung pouf now released below began to sway and push at him. The widow started to unhook the lace herself and Pyotr Ivanovich sat down again, quelling the rebellious pouf underneath him. But the widow hadn't unhooked it all, and Pyotr Ivanovich again got up and the pouf again rebelled and even made a noise. When all this was over she took out a clean cambric handkerchief and began to cry. Pyotr Ivanovich felt chilled by the episode of the lace and the battle with the pouf and sat frowning. This awkward situation was interrupted by Sokolov, Ivan Ilyich's butler, reporting that the place in the cemetery Praskovya Fyodorovna had selected would cost two hundred rubles. She stopped crying and, looking at Pyotr Ivanovich with the air of a victim, said in French that she was suffering greatly. Pyotr Ivanovich made a silent sign expressing a firm conviction that it couldn't be otherwise.

"Do smoke, please," she said in a gracious and, at the same time, broken voice and talked to Sokolov about the matter of the price of the place in the cemetery. Pyotr Ivanovich smoked and heard her asking very detailed questions about the different prices of plots and deciding on the one that should be bought. When that was done, she went on to give instructions about the singers. Sokolov went out.

"I do everything myself," she said to Pyotr Ivanovich, moving some albums lying on the table to one side. Noticing that his ash was posing a threat to the table, she speedily pushed an ashtray towards Pyotr Ivanovich and said, "I find it a pretence to state that because of grief I can't deal with practical matters. On the contrary, if there is something that can . . . not console . . . but distract me, then it's bothering about him." She again took out her handkerchief as if she were going to cry, and suddenly, as if pulling herself together, she shook herself and began to speak quietly:

"However, I have to talk to you about something."

Pyotr Ivanovich bowed, not letting the pouf release its springs, which had at once started to move underneath him.

"He suffered terribly in the last days."

"Did he suffer very much?" Pyotr Ivanovich asked.

"Oh. Terribly! At the end he never stopped screaming, not for minutes, for hours. For three whole days he screamed without drawing breath. It was unbearable. I can't understand how I bore it; one could hear it from three doors away. Oh, what I've been through!"

"And was he really conscious?" Pyotr Ivanovich asked.

"Yes," she whispered, "till the final moment. He said goodbye to us a quarter of an hour before he died and asked as well for Volodya to be taken out."

The thought of the sufferings of a man he had known so well, first as a cheerful lad, a schoolboy, then as an adult colleague, suddenly horrified Pyotr Ivanovich in spite of his unpleasant consciousness of his own and this woman's pretense. He saw again that forehead, the nose pressing on the lip, and he became fearful for himself.

Three days of terrible suffering and death. That can happen to me too, now, any minute, he thought, and for a moment he became frightened. But right away, he didn't know how, there came to his aid the ordinary thought that this had happened to Ivan Ilyich and not to him, and this ought not and could not happen to him; that in thinking like this he was giving in to gloomy thoughts, which one shouldn't, as had been clear from Schwarz's face. And having reached this conclusion, Pyotr Ivanovich was reassured and started to ask with interest about the details of Ivan Ilyich's end, as if death were an adventure peculiar to Ivan Ilyich but absolutely not to himself.

After some talk about the details of the truly terrible physical sufferings which Ivan Ilyich had undergone (details that Pyotr Ivanovich learned only by way of the effect that Ivan Ilyich's torment had had on Praskovya Fyodorovna's nerves), the widow apparently found it necessary to move on to business.

"Ah, Pyotr Ivanovich, it's so hard, so terribly hard." And she again started to cry.

Pyotr Ivanovich sighed and waited for to her to blow her nose. When she had blown her nose, he said:

"Believe me . . ." and again she talked away and unburdened herself of what was clearly her main business with him—how on her husband's death she could get money from the treasury. She gave the appearance of asking Pyotr Ivanovich for advice about the pension, but he saw that she already knew down to the smallest details even what he didn't know—everything that one could extract from the public purse on this death—but that she wanted to learn if one couldn't somehow extract a bit more money. Pyotr Ivanovich tried to think of a way, but, having thought a little and out of politeness abusing the government for its meanness, he said that he thought one couldn't get more. Then she sighed and clearly began to think of a way to get rid of her visitor. He understood this, put out his cigarette, got up, shook her hand, and went into the hall.

In the dining room with the clock that Ivan Ilyich had been so pleased to buy in a junk shop, Pyotr Ivanovich met the priest and also a few acquaintances who had come to the requiem, and he saw a beautiful young lady he knew, Ivan Ilyich's daughter. She was all in black. That made her very slender waist seem even more so. She had a somber, decisive, almost angry expression. She bowed to Pyotr Ivanovich as if he had done something wrong. Behind the daughter, with a similarly offended expression, stood a rich young man whom Pyotr Ivanovich knew, an examining magistrate who he'd heard was her fiancé. He glumly bowed to them and was about to go on into the room where the dead man lay when from under the stairs there appeared the figure of the son, a gymnasium student, who looked terribly like Ivan Ilyich. He was a little Ivan Ilyich just as Pyotr Ivanovich remembered him at law school. His eyes were tearstained and had the look that the eyes of boys with impure thoughts have at the age of thirteen or fourteen. When he recognized Pyotr Ivanovich the boy began to scowl sullenly and shamefacedly. Pyotr Ivanovich nodded to him and went into the dead man's room. The requiem began—candles, groans, incense, tears, sobs. Pyotr Ivanovich stood frowning, looking at the feet in front of him. He didn't look once at the dead man and right until the end didn't give in to any depressing influences. He was one of the first to leave. There was no one in the hall. Gerasim, the peasant manservant, darted out of the dead man's study, rummaged with his strong hands among all the fur coats to find Pyotr Ivanovich's, and gave it to him.

"So, Gerasim my friend," said Pyotr Ivanovich in order to say something. "It's sad, isn't it?"

"It's God's will. We'll all be there," said Gerasim, showing his white, regular, peasant's teeth, and like a man in the full swing of intensive work, briskly opened the door, called the coachman, helped Pyotr Ivanovich in, and jumped back to the steps as if trying to think what else he might do.

It was particularly pleasant for Pyotr Ivanovich to breathe the fresh air after the smells of incense, the dead body, and the carbolic acid.

"Where to, sir?" asked the coachman.

"It's not late. So I'll still drop in at Fyodor Vasilyevich's."

And off Pyotr Ivanovich went. And indeed he found his friends finishing the first rubber; it was easy for him to cut in as a fifth.

II

IVAN ILYICH'S PAST LIFE HAD BEEN VERY SIMPLE AND ordinary and very awful.

Ivan Ilyich had died at the age of forty-five, a member of the Court of Justice. He was the son of a St. Petersburg civil servant who had in various ministries and departments the kind of career that brings people to a position in which, although it is quite clear that they are incapable of performing any meaningful job, they still by reason of their long past service and seniority cannot be dismissed; so they receive invented, fictitious positions and thousands of rubles, from six to ten thousand, which are not fictitious, with which they live on to a ripe old age.

Such was Privy Councillor[4] Ilya Yefimovich Golovin, the superfluous member of various superfluous institutions.

He had three sons, Ivan Ilyich being the second. The eldest had the same kind of career as his father, only in a different ministry, and he was already approaching the age at which salary starts increasing automatically. The third son was a failure. Wherever he had been in various positions he had made a mess of things and he was now working in the railways. Both his father and his brothers, and especially their wives, not only didn't like to see him but didn't even mention his existence unless absolutely compelled to do so. Their sister was married to Baron Gref, the same kind of St. Petersburg civil servant as his father-in-law. Ivan Ilyich was *le phénix de la famille*,[5] as they said. He wasn't as cold and precise as the eldest or as hopeless as the youngest. He was somewhere between them—a clever, lively, pleasant, and decent man. He had been educated with his younger brother in the law school. The younger one didn't finish and was expelled from the fifth class. Ivan Ilyich completed the course with good marks. In law school he was already what he would later be during his entire life: a capable, cheerful, good-natured, and sociable man, but one who strictly did what he considered his duty, and he considered his duty to be everything that it was considered to be by his superiors. Neither as a boy nor afterward as a grown man did he seek to ingratiate himself, but there was in him from a young age the characteristic of being drawn to people of high station like a fly toward the light; he adopted their habits and their views on life and established friendly relations with them. All the passions of childhood and youth went by without leaving much of a trace in him; he gave in both to sensuality and to vanity, and—toward the end, in the senior classes—to liberalism, but always within the defined limits that his sense accurately indicated to him as correct.

At law school he had done things that previously had seemed to him quite vile and had filled him with self-disgust while he did them; but later, seeing these things were done by people in high positions and were not thought by them to be bad, he didn't quite think of them as good but completely forgot them and wasn't at all troubled by memories of them.

Having left law school in the tenth class and received money from his father for fitting himself out, Ivan Ilyich ordered clothes at Sharmer's,[6] hung on his watch chain a medallion with the inscription *respice finem*,[7] took his leave of the princely patron of the school and his tutor, dined with his schoolmates at Donon's,[8] and, equipped with a new and fashionable trunk, linen, clothes, shaving and toilet things, and traveling rug ordered and bought from the very best shops, he went off to a provincial city to the post of assistant to the governor for special projects, which his father had procured for him.

In the provincial city Ivan Ilyich at once established for himself the kind of easy and pleasant position he had had at law school. He worked, made his career, and at the same time amused himself in a pleasant and seemly way; from time to time he went around the district towns on a mission from his chief. He behaved to both superiors and inferiors with dignity and he carried out the responsibilities he had been given, mainly for the affairs of religious dissenters, with an exactness and incorruptible honesty of which he could not but be proud.

In his work, despite his youth and liking for frivolous amusement, he was exceptionally reserved, formal, and even severe; but in society he was often playful and witty and always good-humored, well-behaved and *bon enfant*,[9] as his chief and his chief's wife, with whom he was one of the family, used to say of him.

There was also in the provincial city an affair with one of the ladies who attached herself to the smart lawyer; there was a little dressmaker; there were drinking sessions with visiting aides-de-camp and trips to a remote street after supper; there was also some fawning deference to his chief and even to his chief's wife, but all this wore such a high tone of probity that it couldn't be described in bad words; all this could only go under the rubric of the French expression *il faut que jeunesse se passe*.[10] Everything took place with clean hands, in clean shirts, with French words, and, most importantly, in the highest society, consequently with the approval of people in high position.

Ivan Ilyich worked in this way for five years, and then there came changes in his official life. New legal bodies were founded; new men were needed.

And Ivan Ilyich was this new man.

Ivan Ilyich was offered the position of examining magistrate and he accepted it, despite the fact that this position was in another province and he had to abandon the relationships he had established and establish new ones. His friends saw Ivan Ilyich off: they took a group photograph, they presented him with a silver cigarette case, and off he went to his new position.

As an examining magistrate Ivan Ilyich was just as *comme il faut*,[11] well-behaved, capable of separating his official duties from his private life and of inspiring general respect as he had been as a special projects officer. The actual work of a magistrate had much more interest and attraction for him than his previous work. In his previous position it had been pleasant to walk with a light step in his Sharmer uniform past trembling petitioners and envious officials waiting to be seen, straight into his chief's room to sit down with him over a cup of tea with a cigarette. But there were few people who depended directly on his say-so—only district police officers and religious schismatics when he was sent on missions—and he liked to treat such people dependent on him politely, almost as comrades; he liked to let them feel that here he was, someone who could crush them, treating them in a simple and friendly way. There were only a few such people then. Now, as an examining magistrate, Ivan Ilyich felt that all of them, all without exception, even the most important, self-satisfied people, were in his hands, and that he only had to write certain words on headed paper and this or that important, self-satisfied man would be brought to him as a defendant or a witness, and if he wouldn't let him sit down, would have to stand before him and answer his questions. Ivan Ilyich never abused this power of his—on the contrary he tried to use it lightly—but the consciousness of this power and the possibility of using it lightly constituted for him the chief interest and attraction of his new job. In the work itself, in the actual investigations, Ivan Ilyich very quickly mastered a way of setting aside all circumstances that didn't relate to the investigation and expressing the most complicated case in a terminology in which the case only appeared on paper in its externals and his personal view was completely excluded, and most importantly all requisite formality was observed. This work was something new. And he was one of the first people who worked out the practical application of the statutes of 1864.[12]

Moving to a new city to the post of examining magistrate, Ivan Ilyich made new acquaintances and connections, positioned himself afresh, and adopted a slightly different tone. He positioned himself at a certain respectable distance from the governing authorities, but chose the best circle of the lawyers and nobles who lived in the city and adopted a tone of slight dissatisfaction with government, moderate liberalism, and enlightened civic-mindedness. Moreover, without changing the elegance of his dress, in his new job Ivan Ilyich stopped shaving his chin and let his beard grow freely.

Ivan Ilyich's life turned out very pleasantly in the new city as well: the society that took a critical view of the governor was good and friendly; his salary was larger; and a not inconsiderable pleasure was added to his life by *vint*, which Ivan Ilyich started to play, having an ability to play cards cheerfully, quick-wittedly, and very shrewdly so that generally he won.

After two years working in the new city Ivan Ilyich met his future wife. Praskovya Fyodorovna Mikhel was the most attractive, cleverest, most brilliant girl of the group in which Ivan Ilyich moved. Among the other amusements and relaxations from the labors of a magistrate Ivan Ilyich developed a playful, easy relationship with Praskovya Fyodorovna.

While he had been a special assignments official Ivan Ilyich used to dance as a matter of course; as an examining magistrate he now danced only on special occasions. He danced now in the sense that although he was a part of the new institutions and in the fifth grade,[13] when it came to dancing, then he could show that in this field he could do things better than others. So from time to time at the end of an evening he used to dance with Praskovya Fyodorovna, and it was during these dances in particular that he conquered her. She fell in love with him. Ivan Ilyich didn't have a clear, defined intention of marrying, but when the girl fell in love with him, he asked himself a question. "Actually, why not get married?" he said to himself.

Miss Praskovya Fyodorovna was from a good noble family, was not bad-looking, and had a bit of money. Ivan Ilyich could aspire to a more brilliant match, but this too was a good match. Ivan Ilyich had his salary; she, he hoped, would have as much again. The family connection was good; she was a sweet, pretty, and absolutely decent woman. To say that Ivan Ilyich married because he fell in love with his bride and found in her sympathy for his views on life would have been as unjust as to say that he married because people in his social circle approved of the match. Ivan Ilyich married because of both considerations: he was doing something pleasant for himself in acquiring such a wife, and at the same time he was doing something his superiors thought a right thing to do.

And so Ivan Ilyich married.

The actual process of marriage and the first period of married life, with its conjugal caresses, new furniture, new china, and new linen, went very well until his wife's pregnancy, so that Ivan Ilyich was beginning to think that marriage not only would not destroy the character of an easy, pleasant, cheerful life, one wholly decorous and approved of by society, which Ivan Ilyich thought the true quality of life, but would enhance it further. But then from the first months of his wife's pregnancy something new appeared, something unexpected, unpleasant, oppressive, and indecorous that one couldn't expect and from which one couldn't escape.

His wife for no reason, so Ivan Ilyich thought, as he said to himself, began *de gaieté de coeur*[14] to destroy the pleasant tenor and decorum of life. She was jealous of him without any cause, demanded attentions to herself from him, found fault with everything, and made crude and unpleasant scenes.

At first Ivan Ilyich had hoped to be freed from the unpleasantness of this situation by the same easy and decorous attitude to life which had rescued him before—he tried to ignore his wife's state of mind and continued to live pleasantly and decorously as before: he invited friends home for a game of cards; he tried to go out to his club or see his friends. But on one occasion his wife started to abuse him rudely with such energy and continued to abuse him so persistently every time he didn't fulfill her demands, clearly having made a firm decision not to stop until he would submit—that is, sit at home and be miserable like her—that Ivan Ilyich was horrified. He understood that married life—at any rate with his wife—does not always make for the pleasures and decorum of life but on the contrary often destroys them, and therefore it was essential to protect himself from this destruction. And Ivan Ilyich began to seek the means for this. His official work was one thing that impressed Praskovya Fyodorovna, and Ivan Ilyich through his official work and the duties that arose out of it began to fight his wife, securing his own independent world.

A child was born. There were attempts at feeding and various failures in this, along with the real and imaginary illnesses of child and mother. Sympathy for all this was demanded from Ivan Ilyich but he could understand nothing of it. So the requirement of Ivan Ilyich to fence in a world for himself outside of the family became all the more pressing.

As his wife became more irritable and demanding, so Ivan Ilyich moved the center of gravity of his life more and more into his official work. He came to like his work more and became more ambitious than he had been before.

Very soon, not more than a year after their marriage, Ivan Ilyich understood that married life, which offers certain conveniences, in reality is a very complicated and difficult business with which, in order to do one's duty—that is, to lead a decorous life that is approved of by society—one has to develop a defined relationship as one does with one's work.

And Ivan Ilyich did develop for himself such a relationship with married life. He required of family life only those conveniences it could give him, of dinner at home, a mistress of the house, a bed, and most importantly, that decorum of external appearances which were defined by public opinion. For the rest he looked for cheerfulness and pleasure, and if he found them was very grateful; if he met rejection and querulousness, he at once went off into the separate world of official work that he had fenced in for himself and found pleasure there.

Ivan Ilyich was valued as a good official and in three years he was made assistant prosecutor. His new responsibilities, their importance, the ability to bring anyone to trial and send him to prison, the public nature of his speeches, the success Ivan Ilyich had in this work—all of this tied him even more closely to his official work.

More children came. His wife became more and more querulous and angry, but the relationship Ivan Ilyich had developed with domestic life had made him almost impervious to her querulousness.

After seven years of working in one city Ivan Ilyich was promoted to the position of prosecutor in a different province. They moved; they now had little money and his wife didn't like the place to which they had moved. Though his salary was more than it had been, life cost more; also two children died, and so family life became even more unpleasant for Ivan Ilyich.

Praskovya Fyodorovna blamed her husband for all the misfortunes that befell them in their new home. Most subjects of conversation between husband and wife, particularly the education of the children, led to questions that recalled past disputes, and quarrels were ready to break out at every minute. There remained only rare periods of tenderness that came to the married couple but did not last long. These were islands on which they landed for a while but then again sailed off into the sea of hidden animosity which expressed itself in their alienation from each other. This alienation might have distressed Ivan Ilyich if he had thought that it should not be like this, but he now recognized this situation not just as normal but as the actual goal of his family life. His object was to free himself more and more from these unpleasant things and to give them a character of innocuous decorum; he achieved it by spending less and less time with his family and when he was forced to do it, he tried to protect his situation by the presence of outsiders. The important thing was that Ivan Ilyich had his official work. For him all the interest of life was concentrated in that official world, and this interest absorbed him. The consciousness of his power, of his ability to bring down anyone he chose to, his importance, even in externals when he entered the court and at meetings with subordinates, his mastery of conducting the work—all this made him feel glad, and together with talking to his friends, with dinners and *vint*, it filled up his life. So overall Ivan Ilyich's life continued to go on as he thought that it should: pleasantly and with decorum.

So he lived for another seven years. His elder daughter was now sixteen, another child had died, and there only remained a boy at the gymnasium, a subject of dissension. Ivan Ilyich had wanted to send him to law school but to spite him Praskovya Fyodorovna had sent the boy to the gymnasium. The daughter was taught at home and had grown into a good-looking girl; the boy too wasn't bad at his studies.

III

THAT WAS IVAN ILYICH'S LIFE FOR SEVENTEEN YEARS after his marriage. He was now a senior prosecutor, having refused various promotions in the expectation of a more desirable position, when something very unpleasant happened which completely destroyed the tranquility of his life. Ivan Ilyich was expecting the position of president of the tribunal in a university town, but somehow Hoppe overtook him and got the place. Ivan Ilyich was angry, started to make accusations, and quarreled with him and his closest superiors; they cooled towards him and passed him over for the next appointment.

That was in 1880. That year was the hardest in Ivan Ilyich's life. In that year his salary wasn't sufficient for living; everyone forgot him, and what appeared to him to be the greatest, the cruellest injustice toward him was found by others to be something completely ordinary. Even his father didn't see it as his duty to help him. He felt everyone had abandoned him, considering his situation on a 3,500-ruble salary quite normal and even fortunate. He alone knew that with his consciousness of the injustices done to him, his wife's constant nagging, and the debts he was beginning to run, living above his means—he alone knew that his situation was far from normal.

In the summer of that year, to ease his finances he took some leave and went with his wife to spend the summer at Praskovya Fyodorovna's brother's home.

In the country, without his work, Ivan Ilyich for the first time felt not just boredom but unbearable depression, felt that he could not live like that and that he absolutely had to take some decisive action.

Having spent a sleepless night pacing the terrace, Ivan Ilyich decided to go to Petersburg to make a petition and, in order to punish *them*, those who could not appreciate him, to transfer to another ministry.

The next day, in spite of all the attempts of his wife and brother-in-law to dissuade him, he traveled to Petersburg.

He went for one thing: to obtain a five-thousand-ruble

salary. He was no longer holding out for any particular ministry or direction or type of work. He just needed a position, a position on five thousand rubles, in government, in banking, in the railways, in the Empress Maria's Foundations,[15] even in customs, but he absolutely had to have five thousand rubles and he absolutely had to leave the ministry where they couldn't appreciate him.

And now this trip of Ivan Ilyich's was crowned with amazing, unexpected success. In Kursk he was joined in a first-class carriage by F. S. Ilyin, someone he knew, who told him about a telegram the governor of Kursk had just received that announced a reorganization to take place in the ministry: Pyotr Ivanovich's position was going to be taken by Ivan Semyonovich.

The planned upheaval, apart from its significance for Russia, had a particular significance for Ivan Ilyich: by promoting a new face, Pyotr Petrovich, and of course Zakhar Ivanovich, his classmate and friend, it was highly propitious for him.

In Moscow the news was confirmed. And when he reached Petersburg, Ivan Ilyich found Zakhar Ivanovich and got the promise of a sure place in his old ministry of justice.

After a week he telegraphed his wife: *Zakhar has Miller's place stop I receive position at next report.*

Thanks to this change of personnel Ivan Ilyich got this position in his old ministry, which placed him two ranks above his old colleagues as well as a salary of 5,000 rubles and 3,500 for removal expenses. All his anger against his former enemies and the entire ministry was forgotten, and Ivan Ilyich was altogether happy.

Ivan Ilyich returned to the country more cheerful and content than he had ever been. Praskovya Fyodorovna cheered up too and a truce was established between them. Ivan Ilyich told her how in Petersburg everyone had feted him, how all his old enemies had been shamed and were now crawling before him, how he was envied for his position, and especially how highly he was regarded by everyone in Petersburg.

Praskovya Fyodorovna listened to all this and appeared to believe it, and she didn't contradict him in anything but just made plans for their new life in the city to which they were moving. And Ivan Ilyich joyfully saw that these plans were his plans, that the plans were tallying, and that his life which had faltered was again taking on its true and natural character of cheerful pleasantness and decorum.

Ivan Ilyich had come just for a short time. On September 10 he had to take up the new job and furthermore he needed time to settle in their new home, to move everything from the provincial city, and to buy and order many more things; in a word, to settle as had been decided in his own mind and almost exactly as had been decided in that of Praskovya Fyodorovna.

And now, when everything had worked out so well and he and his wife were agreed about their goals (and furthermore weren't living much together), they got on harmoniously as they hadn't done since the first years of married life. Ivan

Ilyich thought of taking his family away with him immediately but the insistence of his brother-in-law and his wife, who had suddenly become particularly friendly and familial towards Ivan Ilyich and his family, resulted in Ivan Ilyich going away alone.

Ivan Ilyich left, and the cheerful state of mind brought about by his success and the harmony with his wife, one reinforcing the other, stayed with him the whole time. A delightful apartment was found, the very one husband and wife had been dreaming of. High, spacious, old-fashioned reception rooms; a comfortable, imposing study; rooms for his wife and daughter; a schoolroom for his son—everything as if devised purposely for them. Ivan Ilyich set about arranging it himself: he chose wallpaper, he bought more furniture (antiques in particular whose style he found particularly *comme il faut*), he had things upholstered, and it all grew and grew and approached the ideal he had composed for himself. Even when he had half arranged things, his arrangements exceeded his expectation. He understood the *comme il faut* look, elegant without vulgarity, which everything would take on once it was ready. As he went to sleep he imagined to himself how the reception room would be. Looking at the drawing room, which wasn't yet finished, he could already see the fireplace, the screen, the whatnot and the little chairs disposed about the room, the plates and saucers on the walls, and the bronzes all standing in their places. He was pleased by the thought that he would surprise Pasha and Lizanka, his wife and daughter, who also had a taste for this. They were certainly not expecting this. He was particularly successful in finding old things and buying them cheaply; they gave everything a particularly aristocratic air. In his letters he deliberately described everything in less attractive terms than the reality to surprise them. All this absorbed him so much that even his new job absorbed him less than he had expected—though he loved his work. During sittings of the court he had moments of absent mindedness; he started thinking about whether the curtain pelmets should be straight or curved. He was so absorbed by this that he often did things himself; he even moved the furniture about and rehung the curtains himself. Once he got up on a ladder to show a slow-witted decorator how he wanted the drapes hung; he missed his footing and fell, but being a strong and agile man he held his balance and only knocked his side on the handle of the window frame. The bruise was painful but soon disappeared. During all this time Ivan Ilyich felt particularly well and cheerful. He wrote, "I fell I'm fifteen years younger." He thought the work would be finished in September but it dragged on till mid-October. But the apartment was delightful—it wasn't just he who said this but everyone who saw it said so to him.

In actual fact it was the same as the houses of all people who are not so rich but want to be like the rich and so are only like one another: brocade, ebony, flowers, carpets, and bronzes, everything dark and shiny—everything that all people of a certain type do to be like all people of a certain type. And what he had was so like that that one couldn't even notice it, but to him it all looked somehow special. When he met his family at the railway station and took them to his apartment, all finished and lit up, and a manservant in a white tie opened the door into the flower-decked hall, and they went into the drawing room and study, he was very happy, he took them everywhere, drank in their praise, and beamed with pleasure. That evening, when over tea Praskovya Fyodorovna asked him among other things how he had fallen, he laughed and in front of them showed how he had gone flying and frightened the decorator.

"It's lucky I am a gymnast. Someone else might have been killed but I only knocked myself a bit here; when you touch it—it hurts, but it'll pass; it's just a bruise."

And they started to live in the new home which, as always, once they had settled in properly, turned out to have one room too few, with the new income which, as always, turned out to be too little (only not by very much—five hundred rubles). And life was very good. Especially good at first when all was not yet done and more still had to be done: things to be bought, ordered, moved, adjusted. Although there were some disagreements between husband and wife, they were both so pleased and there was so much to do that everything was finished without serious quarrels. When there was nothing left to do, it became a bit more boring and something seemed lacking, but now friendships were made and habits established and life filled up.

After spending the morning in court Ivan Ilyich returned for dinner, and at first his mood was good, although it suffered a little, specifically because of their home. (Every stain on a tablecloth or brocade or broken curtain cord irritated him; he had put in so much work into the arrangement that every disruption of it was painful to him.) But in general Ivan Ilyich's life went on just as in his view life should flow: easily, pleasantly, and decorously. He rose at nine, drank his coffee, read the newspapers, then put on his uniform[16] and drove to the court. There the harness in which he worked was already molded for him and he slipped into it right away: petitioners, chancery inquiries, the chancery itself, public and executive sittings of the court. In all of these one had to know how to exclude anything raw and vital, which always destroys the even flow of official work: one couldn't admit any human relationships except official ones; the occasion for a relationship had to be solely official and so had the relationship itself. For example, a man would come in and want to find out something. Outside his official role Ivan Ilyich could not have any relationship with him; but if this man had a relationship with him as a member of the court, one that could be expressed on headed paper—then within the bounds of this relationship Ivan Ilyich would do everything, absolutely everything he could, and in doing this would observe the semblance of friendly relations, that is, courtesy. As soon as the official relationship was ended, so was any other. This ability to separate out the official side without combining it with his real life Ivan Ilyich possessed in the highest degree, and by his talents and long practice he had developed it to such a point that he even sometimes, like a virtuoso, would allow himself as if in jest to combine personal and official relationships. He would allow himself this because he always felt in himself the power to split off the official again when necessary and to reject the personal. Ivan Ilyich handled this work of his not just easily, agreeably, and decorously but even with the mastery of a virtuoso. Between cases he would smoke, drink tea, chat a bit about politics, a bit about generalities, a bit about cards, and most of all about official appointments. And he would return home tired but with the feeling of a virtuoso who had given a lucid performance of his part, one of the first violins in the orchestra. At home mother and daughter would go out somewhere or someone came to see them; his son was at the gymnasium, preparing his lessons with tutors and diligently studying the things they teach in a gymnasium. Everything was good. After dinner, if there were no guests, Ivan Ilyich would sometimes read a book about which people were talking a lot, and in the evenings he would sit down to his work, that is, read his papers, consult the law, examine testimony, and check it against the law. All this he found neither boring nor amusing. It was boring if he could be playing *vint*; but if there was no *vint*—then all the same this was better than sitting by himself or with his wife. Ivan Ilyich's pleasures were little dinners to which he would invite ladies and gentlemen who were important in terms of worldly position and spending his time with them: that was just like the usual way such people spend their time, just as his drawing room was like all drawing rooms.

Once they even had an evening party, with dancing. And Ivan Ilyich felt cheerful and everything was good, except he had a big quarrel with his wife over the cakes and sweets: Praskovya Fyodorovna had her own plan, but Ivan Ilyich insisted on getting everything from an expensive confectioner and the quarrel was because there were cakes left over and the confectioner's bill came to forty-five rubles. The quarrel was a big and unpleasant one to such a point that Praskovya Fyodorovna called him "an idiot and a misery," and he took his head in his hands and in a fit of temper said something about divorce. But the actual party was enjoyable. The very best society was there and Ivan Ilyich danced with Princess Trufonova, sister of the famous founder of the Goodbye Sorrow Society. His official pleasures were pleasures of pride; his social pleasures were pleasures of vanity; but Ivan Ilyich's real pleasures were the pleasures of playing *vint*. He admitted that after all the various unhappy events in his life the pleasure that burnt like a candle above all others was to sit down at *vint* with good players and partners who didn't shout, definitely in a four (when you're five it's really annoying to have to stand out, although you pretend you very much like it), and to have an intelligent, serious game (when the cards are right), and then to have supper and drink a glass of wine. After *vint*, especially after a little win (a big win was unpleasant), Ivan Ilyich went to bed in an especially good mood.

That's how they lived. They formed around them a group of the best society, important people went to them and young people, too.

Husband, wife, and daughter were agreed in their views of their circle of acquaintances, and without any formal understanding they dropped and were rid of all sorts of shabby little friends and relatives who used to drop in to see them, spouting endearments into the drawing room with Japanese plates hanging on the wall. Soon these shabby little friends stopped dropping in and the Golovins were left with just the very best society. Young men paid court to Lizanka and Petrishchev, an examining magistrate, the son of Dmitry Ivanovich Petrishchev[17] and sole heir to his property, began to pay so much attention to her that Ivan Ilyich even talked about it to Praskovya Fyodorovna. Shouldn't they bring them together in a troika ride or organize some theatricals? That's how they lived. And everything went on like that, without any change, and everything was very good.

IV

THEY WERE ALL IN GOOD HEALTH. ONE COULDN'T CALL poor health the fact that Ivan Ilyich sometimes said he had an odd taste in his mouth and something felt uncomfortable on the left side of his stomach.

But it happened that this discomfort started to grow and to become not quite pain but the consciousness of a constant heaviness in his side accompanied by a bad mood. This bad mood, which got worse and worse, began to spoil the pleasant course of the easy and decorous life that had been established in the Golovin house. Husband and wife began to quarrel more and more often, and soon the ease and pleasantness disappeared and only decorum was preserved, with difficulty. Again scenes became more frequent. Again there remained just some islands of calm, and only a few of those, on which husband and wife could meet without an outburst.

And Praskovya Fyodorovna now said, not without cause, that her husband had a difficult character. With her natural habit of exaggeration she said he had always had this dreadful character, and that one needed her good nature to stand it for twenty years. It was true that the quarrels now started with him. His fault-finding always began just before dinner and often when he was starting to eat, over the soup. He would remark that one of the dishes was damaged, or the food wasn't right, or his son had his elbow on the table, or it was his daughter's hairstyle. And he blamed Praskovya Fyodorovna for everything. At first Praskovya Fyodorovna answered back and was rude to him, but a couple of times at the beginning of dinner he flew into such a rage that she understood this was a morbid condition brought on by the intake of food, so she controlled herself and didn't answer back but ate her dinner quickly. Praskovya Fyodorovna regarded her self-control as greatly to her own credit. Having decided that her husband had a dreadful character and that he had created the unhappiness of her life, she started to feel sorry for herself. And the more she felt sorry for herself, the more she hated her husband. She began to wish that he would die, but she couldn't wish for that because then there would be no salary. And that irritated her even more. She considered herself terribly unhappy precisely because even his death could not rescue her and she became irritated; she concealed it and her concealed irritation increased his own irritation.

After one scene, in which Ivan Ilyich was particularly unfair, and after which in explaining himself he said he was indeed prone to irritability but that it came from his illness, she said to him that if he was ill then he must get treatment, and demanded from him that he see a famous doctor.

He went. Everything was as he had expected; everything happened as it always does. The waiting and the doctor's assumed pompousness, something familiar to him that he knew from himself in court, and the tapping and the auscultation and the questions requiring predetermined and clearly unnecessary answers, and the meaningful air suggesting that you just submit to us, we'll fix everything—we know, we have no doubts about how to fix everything, in the very same way for any man you choose. Everything was precisely as in court. Just as he in court put on an air towards the accused, so in precisely the same way the famous doctor put on an air towards him.

The doctor said: such and such shows that you have such and such inside; but if that isn't confirmed by examining such and such, then one must assume you have such and such. If one does assume such and such, then . . . and so forth. Only one question was important to Ivan Ilyich: was his condition dangerous or not? But the doctor ignored this inappropriate question. From the doctor's point of view the question was pointless and wasn't the one under discussion; it was only a question of assessing various possibilities—a floating kidney, chronic catarrh, or an infection of the appendix. It wasn't a question of Ivan Ilyich's life but an argument between a floating kidney and the appendix. And before Ivan Ilyich's eyes the doctor resolved the argument brilliantly in favor of the floating kidney, with the reservation that an examination of his urine could provide new evidence and then the case would be looked at again. All this was very precisely what Ivan Ilyich himself had done a thousand times with defendants and as brilliantly. The doctor did his summing-up just as brilliantly, triumphantly, even cheerfully, looking at the defendant over his glasses. From the doctor's summing-up Ivan Ilyich drew the conclusion that things were bad, that it didn't matter much to the doctor or probably to anyone else, but that for him things were bad. And Ivan Ilyich was painfully struck by this conclusion that aroused in him a feeling of great self-pity and of great anger toward this doctor who was indifferent to such an important question.

But he didn't say anything and got up, put the money on the desk, and said with a sigh:

"Probably we patients often put inappropriate questions to you. In general terms, is this a dangerous illness or not?"

The doctor gave him one stern look through his glasses as if to say: Accused, if you will not stay within the boundaries of the questions that are put to you, then I will be compelled to give instructions for your removal from the courtroom.

"I have already told you what I consider necessary and proper," said the doctor. "An examination will show the rest." And the doctor bowed.

Ivan Ilyich slowly went out, despondently got into the sleigh, and went home. For the whole journey he ceaselessly went over everything the doctor had said, trying to turn those confused, unclear, scientific words into simple language and to read in them an answer to the question: Am I in a bad way, or a very bad way, or aren't things yet so bad? And he thought that the sense of everything the doctor had said was that he was in a very bad way. Everything in the streets looked sad to Ivan Ilyich. The cab drivers were sad, the houses were sad, the passersby, the shops. This pain, this dull nagging pain that didn't stop for a single second, combined with the doctor's unclear pronouncements acquired another more serious meaning. Ivan Ilyich listened to his pain with a new heavy feeling.

He arrived home and started to tell his wife. His wife listened but in the middle of his account his daughter came in wearing a hat: she and her mother were going out. She sat down for a moment to listen to this boring stuff but she couldn't stand it for long, and her mother didn't listen to the end.

"Now I'm very pleased," his wife said. "So mind you take your medicine properly. Give me the prescription, I'll send Gerasim to the chemist's." And she went to dress.

While she was in the room he was barely able to breathe and he sighed heavily when she went out.

"Well then," he said. "Perhaps it's not so bad."

He began to take the medicines and to follow the doctor's directions, which changed after the urine examination. But it was the case now that there had been some kind of confusion in the examination and in what followed from it. It was impossible to get through to the doctor himself, but it turned out that what was happening was not what the doctor had told him. Either he had forgotten or he had lied or he had concealed something from Ivan Ilyich.

But Ivan Ilyich still started to follow the directions precisely and in doing so at first found some comfort.

From the time he visited the doctor Ivan Ilyich's chief occupations became the precise following of the doctor's directions about hygiene and the monitoring of his pain and all his bodily functions. Ivan Ilyich's chief interests became human illness and human health. When others talked in front of him about people who were ill or had died or had gotten better, and in particular about any illness that resembled his own, he would listen, trying to conceal his agitation, ask questions, and apply what was said to his own illness.

The pain got no less but Ivan Ilyich made an effort to force himself to think he was better. And he could deceive himself as long as nothing disturbed him. But as soon as there was some unpleasantness with his wife or something went wrong at work or he had bad cards at *vint*, he at once felt the full force of his illness. In the past he had endured things going wrong in the expectation that *I'll soon put things right, I'll overcome, I'll be successful, I'll get a grand slam.* Now anything that went wrong brought him down and cast him into despair. He would say to himself, "I was just starting to get better and the medicine was already beginning to work, and along comes this cursed accident or unpleasantness. . . ." And he was angry with the accident or with the people who were causing him unpleasantnesses and killing him, and he felt that this anger was killing him but he couldn't restrain himself. One might have thought it would have been clear to him that this anger against circumstances and people made his illness worse, and that therefore he shouldn't pay any attention to unpleasant incidents, but his reasoning was quite the reverse: He said he needed calm; he watched out for anything that might breach that calm and at the smallest breach he got angry. His condition was made worse by the fact that he consulted medical books and doctors. His deterioration progressed so evenly that comparing one day with another he could deceive himself—there was little difference. But when he consulted doctors, he thought he was getting worse and that very quickly. And in spite of that he constantly consulted doctors.

That month he went see another celebrity doctor; this other celebrity doctor said almost the same as the first but put the questions differently. And consulting this celebrity doctor only deepened Ivan Ilyich's doubt and terror. A friend of a friend—a very good doctor—diagnosed his illness quite differently, and in spite of promising recovery, his questions and assumptions confused Ivan Ilyich even more and increased his doubts. A homeopath diagnosed his illness again quite differently and gave him some medicine, and Ivan Ilyich took it in secret from everyone for about a week. But after a week, feeling no relief and having lost confidence both in the previous treatments and in this one, he fell into greater despair. On one occasion a lady he knew was talking about the healing powers of icons. Ivan Ilyich found himself listening carefully and believing the reality of this. This incident frightened him. "Have I really become so feeble-minded?" he said to himself. "What rubbish! It's all nonsense. I mustn't give in to hypochondria, but having chosen one doctor I must firmly stick to his treatment. That's what I'll do. Now it's settled. I'm not going to think and I'm going to follow the treatment strictly till the summer. Then there'll be something to show. Let's now have an end to all this wavering!" It was easy to say that but impossible to put it into action. The pain in his side wore him down; it seemed to keep getting worse; it became constant; the taste in his mouth became stronger; he thought a disgusting smell was coming from his mouth; and his appetite and strength were going. He couldn't deceive himself: something terrible, new, and important was happening in him, something more important than anything that had happened to Ivan Ilyich in his life. And only he knew about this; all those around him either didn't understand or didn't want to understand and thought that everything in the world was going on as before. That was what tormented Ivan Ilyich most of all. He could see that his household—chiefly his wife and daughter who were in the full swing of visits and parties—understood nothing, and they were vexed that he was so gloomy and demanding, as if he were guilty in that. Although they tried to conceal it, he saw that he was a burden to them, but that his wife had evolved a particular attitude to his illness and adhered to that irrespective of what he said and did. Her attitude was like this:

"You know," she would say to friends, "Ivan Ilyich can't strictly follow a prescribed treatment, as most good people can. Today he'll take his drops and eat what he's been told to and go to bed in good time, but tomorrow if I don't look properly, he'll suddenly forget to take them and eat oysters (which are forbidden him) and sit down to *vint* till one in the morning."

"When did I do that?" Ivan Ilyich would say crossly. "Once at Pyotr Ivanovich's."

"Yesterday with Shebek."

"I just couldn't sleep from the pain . . ."

"Well, whatever it was from, like that you won't get better and you make us miserable."

Praskovya Fyodorovna's public attitude to her husband's illness, which she expressed to others and to him, was that this illness was Ivan Ilyich's own fault and that the whole illness was a new unpleasantness he was bringing down on his wife. Ivan Ilyich felt that this came out in her involuntarily, but that didn't make it any easier for him.

In court Ivan Ilyich noticed or thought he noticed the same strange attitude to him: now he would think that people were scrutinizing him like a man whose position was soon going to be vacant; now all of a sudden his friends would start to joke in an amicable way about his hypochondria, as if this thing, this awful, terrible, unheard-of thing that had grown in him and was ceaselessly gnawing at him and irrepressibly dragging him somewhere, were the most pleasant subject for a joke. He was especially irritated by Schwarz with his playfulness and energy and *comme il faut* ways, all of which reminded Ivan Ilyich of himself ten years back.

Friends came to make up a game; they sat down. They dealt, bending the new cards; he put diamonds next to diamonds, seven of them. His partner bid no trumps—and held two diamonds. What could be better? Things were cheerful and bright—they had a grand slam. And suddenly Ivan Ilyich felt that gnawing pain, that taste in the mouth, and there seemed to him to be something absurd in the fact that he could rejoice in a grand slam.

He looked at Mikhail Mikhaylovich, his partner, rapping his powerful hand on the table and politely and condescendingly refraining from scooping up the tricks but pushing the cards toward Ivan Ilyich to give him the pleasure of picking them up without straining himself and stretching out his arm. "Does he think I'm so weak I can't stretch out my arm?" Ivan Ilyich thought. He forgot about trumps and trumped his partner, losing the grand slam by three tricks—and what was really dreadful was that he saw how Mikhail

Mikhaylovich was suffering, but he didn't care. And it was dreadful to think just why he didn't care.

They all saw he was feeling bad and said to him, "We can stop if you are tired. You must rest." Rest? No, he wasn't tired at all, and they finished the rubber. They were all gloomy and silent. Ivan Ilyich felt he had brought down this gloom upon them and he couldn't dispel it. They had supper and went their ways, and Ivan Ilyich was left alone with the knowledge that his life had been poisoned for him, that it was poisoning the lives of others, and that this poison wasn't losing its power but was penetrating his whole being more and more.

And with this knowledge, with the physical pain, and with the terror, he had to get into bed and often be unable to sleep from the pain the greater part of the night. And the next morning he had to get up again, dress, go to court, talk, write, or if he didn't go to court he had to stay at home with those twenty-four hours of the day, each one of which was a torment. And he had to live like that on the brink of the abyss, all alone, without a single person who could understand and take pity on him.

V

A MONTH WENT BY LIKE THAT AND THEN ANOTHER. Before the new year his brother-in-law came to the city and stayed with them. Ivan Ilyich was in court. Praskovya Fyodorovna had gone out shopping. When Ivan Ilyich went into his study he found his brother-in-law, a healthy, full-blooded fellow, unpacking his suitcase himself. He raised his head when he heard Ivan Ilyich's footsteps and looked at him for a second in silence. That look revealed everything to Ivan Ilyich. His brother-in-law opened his mouth to say "oh" and stopped himself. That movement confirmed everything.

"So, I've changed, haven't I?"

"Yes . . . there is a change."

And however much afterwards Ivan Ilyich turned the conversation with his brother-in-law to his appearance, his brother-in-law said nothing. Praskovya Fyodorovna arrived, his brother-in-law went out to her. Ivan Ilyich locked his door and started to examine himself in the mirror—face-on, then from the side. He took up a photograph of himself with his wife and compared the image with the one he saw in the mirror. The change was huge. Then he bared his arms to the elbow, looked, rolled his sleeves down again, and sat on an ottoman, and his mood became darker than night.

"You mustn't, you mustn't," he said to himself; he jumped up, went to the desk, opened a case file, and began to read it, but he couldn't. He unlocked the door and went into the salon. The drawing-room door was shut. He tiptoed to it and began to listen.

"No, you're exaggerating," said Praskovya Fyodorovna.

"Exaggerating? You don't see—he's a dead man, look at his eyes. There's no light in them. What's the matter with him?"

"Nobody knows. Nikolayev [that was the second doctor] said something, but I don't know what. Leshchetitsky [that was the celebrated doctor] said the opposite . . ."

Ivan Ilyich moved away, went to his room, lay down, and started to think: *A kidney, a floating kidney.* He remembered everything the doctor had told him—how it had become detached and was floating. And with an effort of the imagination he tried to understand his kidney and to halt it and strengthen it; so little was needed for that, he thought. *No, I'll go again to Pyotr Ivanovich.* (That was the friend who had a friend who was a doctor.) He rang, gave orders for the horse to be harnessed, and got ready to leave.

"Where are you off to, *Jean*?"[18] his wife said, using a particularly sad and unusually kind expression.

This unusual kindness angered him. He looked at her morosely.

"I have to go to Pyotr Ivanovich."

He went to his friend who had a friend who was a doctor. He found him at home and had a long conversation with him.

When he considered both the anatomical and physiological details of what, in the doctor's opinion, had been happening inside him, he understood everything.

There was something, a little something in the appendix. All that might be put right. Stimulate the activity of one organ, weaken the activity of another; the something would be absorbed and everything would be put right. He got back a little late for dinner, talked cheerfully for a bit, but for a long time he couldn't go to his room to work. Finally he went into his study and at once sat down to work. He read his cases and worked, but the consciousness that he had set something aside—an important and intimate matter which he would take up once his work was over—did not leave him. When he had finished his cases, he remembered that this intimate matter was his thinking about his appendix. But he didn't indulge it; he went to the drawing room for tea. There were guests, including the examining magistrate, his daughter's intended; they talked and played the piano and sang. Ivan Ilyich spent the evening, as Praskovya Fyodorovna noticed, more cheerfully than he had spent others, but he didn't forget for one minute that he had set aside some important thinking about his appendix. At eleven o'clock he said goodnight and went to his room. Since he had become ill he slept in a little room next to his study. He went in, undressed, and picked up a novel of Zola's, which he didn't read. He began thinking instead. The desired cure of the appendix took place in his imagination. Matter was absorbed, matter was expelled, and normal activity was restored. "Yes, that's how it all is," he said to himself. "Only nature needs a little help." He remembered his medicine, sat up, took it, watching for the beneficial effects of the medicine and the removal of the pain. "Just take it regularly and avoid unhealthy influences; I already feel a bit better, much better." He started to feel his side—it wasn't painful to the touch. "Yes, I can't feel it; I'm really much better now." He put out the candle and lay on his side. "The appendix is getting better; things are being absorbed." Suddenly he felt the familiar old dull nagging pain, the persistent, quiet, serious pain. The familiar nastiness in his mouth. His heart began to pump, his head turned. "My God, my God!" he said. "It's here again, it's here again and it's never going to stop." And suddenly his case presented itself to him from a different perspective. "Appendix! Kidney!" he said to himself. "It's not a case of the appendix or of the kidney, but of life . . . and death. Yes, I had life and now it's passing, passing, and I can't hold it back. That's it. Why deceive oneself? Isn't it obvious to everyone but myself that I am dying, and it's only a question of the number of weeks, days—maybe now. There was light and now there's darkness. I was here but now I'm going there! Where?" A chill came over him, his breathing stopped. He could only hear the beating of his heart.

"I won't exist, so what will exist? Nothing will exist. So where will I be when I don't exist? Is this really death? No, I don't want it." He got up quickly, tried to light a candle, groped with shaking hands, dropped the candle and candlestick on the floor, and slumped back again onto the pillow. "Why? Nothing matters," he said to himself, looking into the darkness with open eyes. "Death. Yes, death. And none of them knows and they don't want to know and they have no pity for me. They're enjoying themselves." Outside the door he could hear the distant noise of music and singing. "They don't care but they too will die. Fools. It'll come to me first, to them later; they too will have the same. But they're having fun, the beasts!" Anger choked him. And he felt painful, unbearable misery. "It cannot be that we're all doomed to this terrible fear." He raised himself.

"Something's not right; I must calm down, I must think over everything from the outset." And he began to think. "Yes, the start of my illness. I knocked my side, and I stayed just the same that day and the next; it ached a bit, then more, then the doctors, then depression, despair, the doctors again; and I kept getting nearer and nearer to the abyss. Less strength. Nearer and nearer. And now I've wasted away, there's no light in my eyes. And death, and I think about my appendix. I think of how to mend my appendix, but this is death. Is it really death?" Again horror came over him; he bent down, tried to find the matches, and banged his elbow on the nighttable. It got in his way and hurt him; he got angry with it; in his irritation he banged his elbow harder and knocked the nighttable over. And in his despair he fell back, gasping for breath, expecting death to come now.

Now the guests were leaving. Praskovya Fyodorovna was seeing them out. She heard something fall and came in.

"What's the matter with you?"

"Nothing. I knocked it over by mistake."

She went out and brought back a candle. He lay breathing heavily and very fast, like a man who has run a mile, looking at her with motionless eyes.

"What's the matter with you, *Jean*?"

"Nothing. I . . . knocked . . . it . . . over." (*What should I say? She won't understand*, he thought.)

Indeed she didn't. She picked the table up, lit a candle for him, and quickly went out; she had to see a guest out.

When she returned, he was lying in the same position, on his back, looking up.

"How are you feeling? Is it worse?"

"Yes, it is."

She shook her head and sat down.

"You know, *Jean*, I am wondering whether we shouldn't ask Leshchetitsky to the house."

That meant asking the celebrated doctor regardless of cost. He smiled venomously and said, "No." She sat for a while, then went over to him and kissed him on the forehead.

When she kissed him he hated her with all his might and made an effort not to push her away.

"Good night. With God's help you'll go to sleep."

"Yes."

VI

IVAN ILYICH SAW THAT HE WAS DYING AND WAS IN CONstant despair.

Ivan Ilyich knew in the very depths of his soul that he was dying but not only could he not get accustomed to this, he simply didn't understand it; he just couldn't understand it.

All his life the example of a syllogism he had studied in Kiesewetter's[19] logic—"Caius is a man, men are mortal, therefore Caius is mortal"—had seemed to him to be true only in relation to Caius but in no way to himself. There was Caius the man, man in general, and it was quite justified, but he wasn't Caius and he wasn't man in general, and he had always been something quite, quite special apart from all other beings; he was Vanya,[20] with Mama, with Papa, with Mitya and Volodya, with his toys and the coachman, with Nyanya, then with Katenka, with all the joys, sorrows, passions of childhood, boyhood, youth. Did Caius know the smell of the striped leather ball Vanya loved so much? Did Caius kiss his mother's hand like that and did the silken folds of Caius's mother's dress rustle like that for him? Was Caius in love like that? Could Caius chair a session like that?

And Caius is indeed mortal and it's right that he should die, but for me, Vanya, Ivan Ilyich, with all my feelings and thoughts—for me it's quite different. And it cannot be that I should die. It would be too horrible.

That's what he felt.

"If I had to die like Caius, then I would know it, an inner voice would be telling me, but nothing like that happened in me, and I and all my friends—we understood that things weren't at all like with Caius. But now there's this!" he said to himself. "It can't be. It can't be, but it is. How has this happened? How can one understand it?"

And he couldn't understand it and tried to banish this

thought as false, inaccurate, morbid, and to replace it with other true and healthy thoughts. But this thought, and not just the thought but reality as it were came and stopped in front of him.

And in the place of this thought he called up others in turn in the hope of finding support in them. He tried to return to his previous ways of thought, which had concealed the thought of death from him. But—strangely—everything which previously had concealed and covered up and obliterated the awareness of death now could no longer produce this result. Ivan Ilyich now spent most of his time attempting to restore his previous ways of feeling that had concealed death. Now he would say to himself, "I'll take up some work, that's what I live by." And he went to court, banishing all his doubts; he talked to friends and sat down, absentmindedly looking over the crowd of people with a pensive look as he used to and supporting both wasted hands on the arms of his oak chair; leaning over toward a friend as usual, moving the papers of a case, whispering together, and then suddenly raising his eyes and sitting up straight, he would pronounce the particular words and open the case. But suddenly in the middle of it, the pain in his side, ignoring the stages of the case's development, began its own gnawing work. Ivan Ilyich listened and tried not to think about it, but it kept on. It came and stood right in front of him and looked at him, and he became petrified; the fire in his eyes died down, and he again began to ask himself, "Is it alone the truth?" And his friends and staff saw with surprise and dismay that he, such a brilliant, subtle judge, was getting confused and making mistakes. He would give himself a shake, make an effort to recover himself, and somehow or other bring the session to an end, and he would return home with the depressing awareness that his work as a judge couldn't hide from him as it used to what he wanted it to hide; that with his work as a judge he couldn't be rid of It. And what was worst of all was that It was distracting him not to make him do anything but only for him to look at It, right in the eye, look at it and without doing anything endure inexpressible sufferings.

And to rescue himself from this condition, Ivan Ilyich looked for relief—for new screens—and new screens appeared and for a short time seemed to offer him salvation, but very soon they again not so much collapsed as let the light through, as if It penetrated everything and nothing could hide it.

Latterly he would go into the drawing room he had arranged—the drawing room where he had fallen—how venomously comic it was to think of it—for the arrangement of which he had sacrificed his life, for he knew that his illness had started with that injury; he would go in and see that something had made a scratch on a polished table. He would look for the cause and find it in the bronze ornament of an album that had become bent at the edge. He would pick up the album, an expensive one he had lovingly compiled, and be cross at the carelessness of his daughter and her friends—things were torn and the photographs bent. He would carefully set things to rights and bend the decoration back again.

He then would have the thought of moving this whole *éstablissement*[21] of albums over into another corner by the flowers. He would call the manservant; either his daughter or his wife would come to his help; they would disagree, contradict him; he would argue, get angry, but everything would be all right because he didn't remember It, couldn't see It.

And then his wife would say when he himself was moving something, "Let the servants do it, you'll hurt yourself again," and suddenly It would flash through the screens; he would see It flash just for a moment, and he still would hope It would disappear, but without wanting to he would pay attention to his side—the same thing would still be sitting there, still aching, and he couldn't forget it, and It would be looking at him quiet openly from behind the flowers. Why?

It's true, it was here on these curtains that I lost my life as if in an assault. Did I really? How terrible and how stupid! It can't be so! It can't be, but it is.

He would go into his study, lie down, and be left alone with It. Face-to-face with It, but nothing to be done with It. Just look at It and turn cold.

VII

HOW IT HAPPENED IN THE THIRD MONTH OF IVAN ILYich's illness is impossible to say because it happened step by step, imperceptibly, but it did happen that his wife and his daughter and his son and the servants and his friends and the doctors and, above all, he himself knew that all interest others had in him lay solely in whether he would soon, at last, vacate his place, free the living from the constraint brought about by his presence, and be liberated himself from his sufferings.

He slept less and less; they gave him opium and started to inject morphine. But that gave him no relief. The dull pangs he felt in his half-somnolent state at first gave him relief as being something new, but then they became as agonizing as outright pain or even more so.

They prepared special food to the doctors' prescriptions, but this food he found more and more tasteless, more and more disgusting.

Special contrivances had to be made for excretion, and every time this was a torment for him. A torment because of the uncleanliness, the loss of decorum, and the odor, from the consciousness that another person had to take part in this.

But some comfort for Ivan Ilyich did come out of this unpleasant business. Gerasim, the manservant, always came to take things out for him.

Gerasim was a clean, fresh young peasant who had filled out on city food. He was always cheerful and sunny. At first Ivan Ilyich was embarrassed by seeing this man, always dressed in his clean, traditional clothes, having to do this repulsive job.

Once getting up from the pan and lacking the strength to pull up his trousers, he collapsed into an easy chair and looked with horror at his feeble bare thighs with their sharply defined muscles.

Gerasim came in with firm, light steps in his heavy boots, giving off a pleasant smell of tar from the boots and of fresh winter air; he had on a clean hessian apron and a clean cotton shirt, the sleeves rolled up over his strong, young, bare arms; without looking at Ivan Ilyich, he went to the vessel, obviously masking the joy in living shining out from his face so as not to hurt the sick man.

"Gerasim," Ivan Ilyich said weakly.

Gerasim started, obviously scared he had made some mistake, and with a quick movement turned toward the sick man his fresh, kind, simple, young face, which was just beginning to grow a beard.

"Do you need something, sir?"

"I think this must be unpleasant for you. You must forgive me. I can't manage."

"No, sir." Gerasim's eyes were shining and he showed his young white teeth. "What's a little trouble? You've got an illness."

And with strong, dexterous hands he did his usual job and went out, treading lightly. And in five minutes, treading just as lightly, he came back.

Ivan Ilyich was still sitting there like that in the armchair.

"Gerasim," he said when Gerasim had put down the clean, rinsed vessel, "please, come here and help me." Gerasim came. “Lift me up. It’s difficult by myself and I’ve sent Dmitry away.”

Gerasim came over to him; he put his strong arms around him and, gently and deftly, the same way he walked, lifted and supported him; he pulled up his trousers with one hand and was going to sit him down. But Ivan Ilyich asked Gerasim to take him to the sofa. Effortlessly and with next to no pressure, Gerasim led him, almost carrying him, to the sofa and sat him down.

“Thank you. How easily, how well . . . you do everything.”

Gerasim again smiled and was about to go out. But Ivan Ilyich felt so good with him around that he didn’t want to let him go.

“Now. Please move this chair over to me. No, that one, underneath my legs. I feel better when my legs are higher.”

Gerasim brought the chair, placed it without making any noise, lowering it in one movement to the floor, and lifted Ivan Ilyich’s legs onto the chair; Ivan Ilyich thought he felt better the moment Gerasim raised up his legs.

“I feel better when my legs are higher,” Ivan Ilyich said. “Put that cushion under me.”

Gerasim did that. Again he lifted his legs up and put the cushion into position. Again Ivan Ilyich felt better when Gerasim held his legs up. When he lowered them, he thought he felt worse.

“Gerasim,” he said to him, “are you busy now?”

“No sir, not at all,” said Gerasim, who had learned from the townsfolk how to talk to the gentry.

"What do you still have to do?"

"What is there to do? I've done everything; I've just got to chop the wood for tomorrow."

"So hold my legs up a bit higher, can you do that?"

"Of course I can." Gerasim lifted up his legs and Ivan Ilyich thought that in this position he felt absolutely no pain.

"But what about the wood?"

"Don't worry, sir. We'll manage."

Ivan Ilyich told Gerasim to sit down and hold up his legs, and he talked to him. And—strange to say—he thought he felt better while Gerasim held up his legs.

From that day Ivan Ilyich started sometimes to call Gerasim in to him and made him hold up his legs on his shoulders, and he liked to talk to him. Gerasim did this easily, willingly, simply, and with a goodness of heart that touched Ivan Ilyich. In all other people Ivan Ilyich was offended by health, strength, high spirits; only Gerasim's strength and high spirits didn't depress but calmed Ivan Ilyich.

Ivan Ilyich's chief torment was the lie—that lie, for some reason recognized by everyone, that he was only ill but not dying, and that he only needed rest and treatment and then there would be some very good outcome. But he knew that whatever they did, there would be no outcome except even more painful suffering and death. And he was tormented by this lie; he was tormented by their unwillingness to acknowledge what everyone knew and he knew, by their wanting to lie to him about his terrible situation, by their wanting him to and making him take part in that lie himself. The lie, this lie being perpetrated above him on the eve of his death, the lie which could only bring down this terrible solemn act of his death to the level of all their visits and curtains and sturgeon for dinner . . . was horribly painful for Ivan Ilyich. And, strangely, many times when they were performing their tricks above him, he was within a hair's breadth of crying out to them, "Stop lying; you know and I know that I am dying; so at least stop lying." But he never had the strength to do it. The terrible, horrific act of his dying, he saw, had been brought down by all those surrounding him to the level of a casual unpleasantness, some breach of decorum (as one treats a man who, entering a drawing room, emits a bad smell); brought down by that very "decorum" he had served his whole life, he saw that no one had pity for him because no one even wanted to understand his situation. Only Gerasim understood his situation and felt pity for him. And so Ivan Ilyich only felt comfortable with Gerasim. He felt comfortable when Gerasim held up his legs, sometimes for whole nights without a break, and wouldn't go off to bed, saying, "Please, sir, don't worry, Ivan Ilyich, I'll still get plenty of sleep"; or when he would suddenly add, going over to the familiar "thou," "You're sick, so why shouldn't I do something for you?" Gerasim was the only one not to lie; everything showed he was the only one who understood what the matter was and didn't think it necessary to hide it, and simply felt pity for his wasted, feeble master.

He even once said directly when Ivan Ilyich was dismissing him:

"We'll all die. So why not take a little trouble?" He said this, conveying by it that he wasn't bothered by the work precisely because he was doing it for a dying man and hoped that in his time someone would do this work for him.

Apart from this lie, or as a consequence of it, what was most painful for Ivan Ilyich was that no one had pity on him as he wanted them to have pity; at some moments after prolonged sufferings Ivan Ilyich wanted most of all, however much he felt ashamed to admit it, for someone to have pity on him like a sick child. He wanted them to caress him, to kiss him, to cry over him as one caresses and comforts children. He knew he was an important legal official, that he had a graying beard and that therefore this was impossible, but he still wanted it. And in his relations with Gerasim there was something close to that, and therefore his relations with Gerasim comforted him. Ivan Ilyich would want to cry, would want them to caress him and cry over him; then in would come his friend, the lawyer Shebek, and instead of crying and caresses Ivan Ilyich would assume a serious, stern, pensive expression and out of inertia would give his opinion on the meaning of a verdict of the court of appeal and stubbornly insist on it. This lie all around him and inside him more than anything poisoned the last days of Ivan Ilyich's life.

VIII

IT WAS MORNING. IT WAS MORNING ONLY BECAUSE GERasim had gone out and Pyotr the manservant came in, put out the candles, opened one curtain, and started quietly to tidy up. Whether it was morning or evening, Friday or Sunday, was immaterial, it was all one and the same: the gnawing, agonizing pain that didn't abate for a moment; the consciousness of life departing without hope but still not yet departed; the same terrible, hateful death advancing, which was the only reality, and always the same lie. What did days, weeks, and times of day matter here?

"Would you like some tea?"

He has to have order; masters should drink tea in the mornings, he thought and only said:

"No."

"Would you like to move to the sofa?"

He has to tidy the chamber, and I'm in the way; I am dirt, disorder, he thought and only said:

"No, leave me be."

The manservant did some more things. Ivan Ilyich stretched out his hand. Pyotr came up to serve.

"What do you want?"

"My watch."

Pyotr got the watch, which was lying right there, and handed it to him.

"Half past eight. Have they got up?"

"No, sir. Vasily Ivanovich"—that was his son—"has gone to the gymnasium, but Praskovya Fyodorovna gave orders to wake her if you asked for her. Shall I?"

"No, don't." *Shall I try some tea?* he thought. "Yes, tea . . . bring it."

Pyotr went to the door. Ivan Ilyich felt terrified of being left alone. *How can I detain him? Yes, my medicine.* "Pyotr, give me my medicine." *Why not, maybe the medicine will still help.* He took the spoon and drank. *No, it won't help. It's all nonsense and a sham,* he decided as soon as he sensed the familiar sickly, hopeless taste. *No, I can't believe in it any more. But the pain, why the pain, if it would just go down even for a minute.* And he groaned. Pyotr turned round again. "No, go away. Bring me some tea."

Pyotr went out. Left alone, Ivan Ilyich groaned not so much from the pain, however frightful it was, as from anguish. "Always the same, always these endless days and nights. If only it could be soon. What could be soon? Death, darkness. No, no. Anything is better than death!"

When Pyotr came in with the tea on a tray, Ivan Ilyich looked distractedly at him for a long time, not taking in who and what he was. Pyotr was embarrassed by this stare. And when Pyotr was embarrassed, Ivan Ilyich came to himself.

"Yes," he said, "tea . . . good, put it down. Only help me wash and give me a clean shirt."

And Ivan Ilyich began to wash. Stopping to rest, he washed his hands, his face, cleaned his teeth, began to brush his hair, and looked in the mirror. He felt frightened, especially frightened by the way his hair stuck flat to his forehead.

When his shirt was being changed, he knew that he would be even more frightened if he looked at his body, and so he didn't look at himself. But now it was all done. He put on a dressing gown, covered himself with a blanket, and sat in an armchair to have his tea. For one minute he felt refreshed, but as soon as he began to drink the tea, again the same taste, the same pain. With an effort he finished the tea and lay down, stretching out his legs. He lay down and sent Pyotr away.

Always the same. There'd be a small flash of hope, then a sea of despair would surge, and always pain, always pain, always despair, and always the same. It was horribly depressing being alone; he wanted to ask for someone but he knew in advance that with others there it would be even worse. "If only I could have morphine again—and lose consciousness. I'll tell him, the doctor, to think of something else. Like this it's impossible, impossible."

An hour, a couple of hours would go by like that. But now there's a bell in the hall. Maybe it's the doctor. It is; it's the doctor, fresh, bright, plump, cheerful, his expression saying, "You've gotten frightened of something there but now we'll fix all that for you." The doctor knows that this expression isn't appropriate here, but he has assumed it once and for all and he can't take it off, like a man who has put on a tailcoat in the morning and is paying visits.

The doctor rubs his hands briskly and reassuringly.

"I'm cold. There's a cracking frost. Let me warm myself up," he says, his expression being as if one just had to wait a little for him to warm himself, and when he had, then he would set everything to rights.

"So, how are we?"

Ivan Ilyich feels the doctor wants to say, "How are things?" but feels one can't talk like that, and he says, "How did you spend the night?"

Ivan Ilyich looks at the doctor, his expression asking, "Will you really never be ashamed of telling lies?" But the doctor doesn't want to understand the question.

And Ivan Ilyich says:

"Just as dreadfully. The pain isn't going, it isn't going away. If I could just have something!"

"Yes, you patients are always like that. Well, sir, now I've warmed up, even our very particular Praskovya Fyodorovna wouldn't have anything to say against my temperature. So, sir, good morning." And the doctor shakes his hand.

And, dropping all his earlier playfulness, the doctor begins to examine the patient with a serious expression, takes pulse and temperature, and then begin the tappings and auscultations.

Ivan Ilyich knows firmly and without any doubt that all this is nonsense, an empty fraud, but when the doctor on his knees stretches over him, applying his ear first higher, then lower, and performs over him various gymnastic exercises, Ivan Ilyich succumbs to all this as he used to succumb to lawyers' speeches when he knew very well that they were lying and why they were lying.

The doctor, kneeling on the sofa, was still tapping something when there was a rustling at the door of Praskovya Fyodorovna's silk dress, and they could hear her scolding Pyotr for not informing her of the doctor's arrival.

She comes in, kisses her husband, and at once starts to make it clear that she has got up long ago and that it's because of a misunderstanding that she wasn't there when the doctor came.

Ivan Ilyich looks at her, examines her closely, and holds against her the whiteness and plumpness and cleanliness of her arms and neck, the gloss of her hair and the shine of her eyes that are so full of life. He hates her with his whole soul. And her touch makes him suffer from a surge of hatred towards her.

Her attitude to him and to his illness is always the same. Just as the doctor has developed for himself an attitude toward his patients which he hasn't been able to put aside, so has she developed a simple attitude towards him—he isn't doing something he should be doing, and it's his fault, and she lovingly scolds him for this—and she hasn't yet managed to put this attitude toward him aside.

"He just doesn't listen. He doesn't take his medicine when he should. And above all—he lies in a position that has to be bad for him—with his legs up."

She described how he makes Gerasim hold his legs.

The doctor smiled a smile of amiable scorn, as if saying, "What can one do? Sometimes these patients dream up such silly things; but one can forgive them."

When the examination was over the doctor looked at his watch, and then Praskovya Fyodorovna announced to Ivan Ilyich that whatever he might want, today she had asked in a famous doctor and he and Mikhail Danilovich (that was the usual doctor's name) would examine him together and discuss the case.

"So please don't go against this. I'm doing this for myself," she said ironically, letting him understand that she did everything for him and just by her saying this he was given no right to refuse her. He said nothing and frowned. He felt that the lies surrounding him had become so tangled that it was difficult now to see anything clearly.

Everything she did for him she did only for herself, and she told him so, as if that was something so unlikely that he had to understand it in the opposite sense.

Indeed the famous doctor did arrive at half past eleven. Again there started the auscultations and serious conversations, both in front of Ivan Ilyich and in another room, about his kidney and appendix, and questions and answers delivered with such a serious air that again, instead of the real question about life and death which now was the only one that confronted him, there came a question about his kidney and appendix, which were doing something not quite as they should be and which Mikhail Danilovich and the celebrity doctor would get to grips with right away and make them correct themselves.

The famous doctor said his goodbyes with a serious expression, but one that hadn't given up hope. And to the timid question Ivan Ilyich put to him, raising eyes that were shining with fear and hope—is there any possibility of recovery?—he answered that though one couldn't guarantee it, there was a possibility. The look of hope with which Ivan Ilyich said goodbye to the doctor was so pitiful that, when she saw it, Praskovya Fyodorovna burst into tears as she went through the study doors to give the famous doctor his fee.

The rise in his spirits brought about by the doctor's encouragement didn't last long. Again it was the same room, the same pictures, curtains, wallpaper, medicine bottles, and his same hurting, suffering body. And Ivan Ilyich started to groan; they gave him an injection and he lost consciousness.

When he came to, it was beginning to get dark; they brought in his dinner. With some effort he took some broth; and again all those same things and again night was coming on.

After dinner at seven o'clock Praskovya Fyodorovna came into his room dressed for an evening out, her breasts large and lifted and traces of powder on her face. That morning she had reminded him that they were going to the theater. Sarah Bernhardt[22] was visiting and they had a box which Ivan Ilyich had insisted they take. Now he had forgotten that, and her clothes outraged him. But he concealed his outrage when he remembered that he himself had insisted they get a box and go because it was a cultural treat for their children.

Praskovya Fyodorovna came in pleased with herself but also with a kind of guilty feeling. She sat down, asked about his health—as he could see, just for the sake of asking rather than to learn, knowing that there was nothing to learn—and began to say what she needed to: that she wouldn't have gone out for anything but the box was taken and Hélène was going and their daughter and Petrishchev (the examining magistrate, their daughter's fiancé), and it was impossible to let them go alone. But it would be so much more agreeable for her to sit with him. He must just do what the doctor had ordered without her.

"Yes, and Fyodor Petrovich[23]—the fiancé—wanted to come in. Can he? Liza, too."

"Let them come in."

His daughter came in all dressed up with her young body bared, that body which made him suffer so. But she was flaunting it. Strong, healthy, clearly in love and angry at the illness, suffering, and death that stood in the way of her happiness.

Fyodor Petrovich came too, in a tailcoat, his hair curled à la Capoul,[24] his long sinewy neck encased in a white collar, with a huge white shirtfront and with powerful thighs squeezed into narrow black trousers, with one white glove pulled onto his hand and an opera hat.

After him the schoolboy crept in inconspicuously in a new school uniform, poor fellow, wearing white gloves and with terrible dark patches under his eyes, the meaning of which Ivan Ilyich knew.

His son always made him feel sorry for him. And the look he gave him was terrible, full of sympathy and fear. Apart from Gerasim, only Vasya understood him and felt pity for him, so Ivan Ilyich thought.

They all sat down, asked again about his health. A silence fell. Liza asked her mother about the opera glasses. There ensued an argument between mother and daughter about who had put them where. It felt unpleasant.

Fyodor Petrovich asked Ivan Ilyich if he had seen Sarah Bernhardt. At first Ivan Ilyich didn't understand what he was being asked and then said:

"No, but have you?"

"Yes, in *Adrienne Lecouvreur*."[25]

Praskovya Fyodorovna said that she was particularly good in something or other. Their daughter disagreed. There began a conversation about the elegance and realism of her acting—that conversation which is always exactly the same.

In the middle of the conversation Fyodor Petrovich looked at Ivan Ilyich and fell silent. The others looked and fell silent. Ivan Ilyich looked straight ahead with shining eyes, clearly becoming angry with them. This had to be put right, but it was quite impossible to put right. Somehow this silence had to be broken. No one had the resolve, and they all became frightened that somehow the decorous lie would collapse and the true state of things would become obvious to all. Liza was the first to take the resolve. She broke the silence. She wanted to hide what they were all feeling, but she said it wrong.

"So, *if we are going to go*, it's time," she said, looking at her watch, a present from her father, and she gave a barely perceptible smile to the young man, which meant something known to them alone, and got up, her dress rustling.

They all got up, said goodbye, and went off.

When they had gone out, Ivan Ilyich thought he felt better: the lie wasn't there—it had gone out with them—but the pain remained. The same constant pain, the same constant fear made nothing more difficult, nothing easier. Everything was worse.

Again minute followed minute, hour followed hour; it was always the same and there was still no end and the inevitable end became more terrifying.

"Yes, send me Gerasim," he said in reply to a question Pyotr asked.

IX

HIS WIFE CAME BACK LATE AT NIGHT. SHE WALKED ON tiptoe but he heard her; he opened his eyes and quickly shut them again. She wanted to send Gerasim away and sit with him herself. He opened his eyes and said:

"No. Go away."

"Are you in a lot of pain?"

"It doesn't matter."

"Take some opium."

He agreed and drank. She went out.

Till three o'clock he was in a tormented stupor. He thought that in some way they were pushing him and his pain into a narrow, deep, black sack; they kept pushing further but they couldn't push them right in. And this terrible business for him was crowned by his suffering. And he was both struggling and wanting to drop right down, both fighting against it and assisting. And suddenly he was free and fell and came to. The same Gerasim was still sitting on the bed at his feet, dozing quietly, patiently. And Ivan Ilyich was lying there, having lifted his emaciated legs in their socks onto Gerasim's shoulders; there was the same candle with its shade and the same unceasing pain.

"Go, Gerasim," he whispered.

"It doesn't matter, sir, I'll sit a bit longer."

"No, go."

He removed his legs and lay on his side on top of his arm, and he began to feel sorry for himself. He waited for Gerasim to go out into the next room and he couldn't control himself anymore, and he burst into tears like a child. He wept for his helplessness, for his horrible loneliness, for people's cruelty, for God's cruelty, for God's absence.

"Why have you done all this? Why have you brought me here? Why, why do you torment me so horribly?"

He didn't expect an answer, but he also wept because there wasn't and couldn't be an answer. The pain increased again but he didn't move or call anyone. He said to himself, "More, go on, beat me! But why? What have I done to you, why?"

Then he calmed down; he not only stopped weeping, he stopped breathing and became all attention, as if he were listening not to a voice speaking in sounds but to the voice of his soul, to the train of thoughts rising within him.

"What do you want?" was the first clear idea capable of being expressed in words that he heard. "What do you want? What do you want?" he repeated to himself. "What? Not to suffer. To live," he answered.

And again he became absorbed with such intense attention that even the pain did not distract him.

"To live? To live how?" asked the voice of his soul.

"Yes, to live, as I lived before: well and pleasantly."

"As you lived before, well, pleasantly?" asked the voice. And he began to go over in his imagination the best moments of his pleasant life. But—strange to relate—all these best moments of a pleasant life now seemed quite different from what they had seemed then. All of them—except for his first memories of childhood. There in childhood was something so truly pleasant with which he could live, if it returned. But the person who had experienced those pleasant things no longer existed: it was like a memory of something else.

As soon as the process began which had resulted in Ivan Ilyich, the man of today, all the things which had seemed joys melted away before his eyes and were changed into something worthless and often vile.

And the further from childhood, the nearer to the present, the more worthless and dubious were the joys. That began with law school. There was still something there truly good: there was gaiety, there was friendship, there were hopes. But in the senior classes these good moments were already less frequent. After that, at the time of his first period of service with the governor, again good moments appeared: there were memories of love for a woman. After that all this became confused and there was even less of what was good. Further on there was still less good, and the further he went the less there was.

Marriage . . . so casually entered, and disillusionment, and the smell that came from his wife's mouth, and sensuality, hypocrisy! And that deadly work of his and those worries about money, and on for a year, and two, and ten, and twenty—and always the same. And the further he went, the more deadly it became. "As if I were walking downhill at a regular pace, imagining I was walking uphill. That's how it was. In the eyes of the world I was walking uphill, and to just that extent life was slipping away from under me. . . And now it's time, to die!

"So what is this? Why? It can't be. It can't be that life was so meaningless and vile. But if it was indeed so meaningless and vile, then why die and die suffering? Something is wrong.

"Maybe I have lived not as I should have"—the thought suddenly came into his head. "But how so when I did everything in the proper way?" he said to himself, and immediately rejected this solution of the whole riddle of life as something wholly impossible.

"What do you want now? To live? To live how? To live

as you lived in court when the court officer pronounces, 'The court is opening!' The court is opening, opening, the court," he repeated to himself. "Here's the court! But I'm not guilty!" he shouted angrily. "For what?" And he stopped weeping and, turning his face to the wall, he began to think of just the one thing: why all this horror, for what?

But however much he thought, he found no answer. And when there came to him the thought, as it often did, that all this was happening because he had lived wrongly, he at once remembered all the correctness of his life and rejected this strange thought.

X

TWO MORE WEEKS WENT BY. IVAN ILYICH DIDN'T GET up from the sofa anymore. He didn't want to lie in bed and instead lay on the sofa. And, lying almost all the time with his face to the wall, he suffered in his loneliness all those same insoluble sufferings and in his loneliness thought the same insoluble thoughts. What is this? Is it really true that this is death? And a voice within answered: Yes, it's true. Why these torments? And the voice answered: That's the way it is; there is no why. Apart from that there was nothing more.

From the very start of his illness, when Ivan Ilyich went to the doctor for the first time, his life was divided into two diametrically opposed moods, which alternated with each other: on the one hand despair and the expectation of an incomprehensible and horrible death, on the other hope and the absorbed observation of the activity of his body. Now he had before his eyes just a kidney or appendix which for a time had deviated from the performance of its duties; now there was just incomprehensible, horrible death from which it was impossible to escape in any way.

From the very beginning of his illness these two moods alternated with each other; but the more the illness progressed, the more fantastic and questionable became thoughts about his kidney and the more real the consciousness of approaching death.

He only had to remember what he had been three months previously and what he was now—to remember how he had been walking downhill at a regular pace—for all possibility of hope to crumble.

In the recent loneliness in which he found himself, lying with his face to the back of the sofa, loneliness in the midst of a crowded city and his numerous acquaintances and family—loneliness that could not be more absolute anywhere, either at the bottom of the sea or underneath the earth—in his recent terrible loneliness Ivan Ilyich lived only by his imagination in the past. One after another pictures of his past presented themselves to him. It always began with the closest in time and went back to the most remote, to his childhood, and rested there. If Ivan Ilyich thought of the stewed prunes he was offered to eat now, he remembered the moist, wrinkled French prunes of his childhood, their particular taste and the flow of saliva when he got to the stone, and alongside this memory of taste there arose a whole row of memories of that time: his *nyanya*, his brother, his toys. "You mustn't think of that. . . . It's too painful," Ivan Ilyich said to himself, and was again transported into the present. A button on the back of the sofa and the creases in its morocco leather. "Morocco is expensive and wears badly; there was a quarrel because of it. But it was different leather and a different row when we ripped our father's briefcase and were punished, but Mama brought us some pies." And again he stopped in his childhood and again it was painful for Ivan Ilyich, and he tried to push it away and think of something else.

And here again, together with this train of memories, another train of memories went through his mind—of how his illness had intensified and grown. It was the same; the further back he went, the more life there was. There was more good in life and more of life itself. And the two merged together. *As my torments kept getting worse and worse, so the whole of life became worse and worse*, he thought. One bright spot, there, at the start of his life, and after that everything blacker and blacker, and everything quicker and quicker. *In inverse ratio to the square of the distance from death*, thought Ivan Ilyich. And an image of a stone flying downward with increasing speed became fixed in his mind. Life, a sequence of increasing sufferings, flies quicker and quicker to the end, to the most terrible suffering of all. *I am flying* . . . He shivered, moved, tried to resist, but he now knew that resistance was impossible, and again, with eyes that were tired of looking but which couldn't help looking at what was in front of him, he gazed at the back of the sofa and waited—waited for that terrible fall, the crash, and annihilation. "I can't resist," he said to himself. "But if I could just understand why. That too I can't. I might be able to explain it if I said I had lived not as I should have. But it's impossible to admit that," he said to himself, remembering all the lawfulness, the correctness, and the decorum of his life. "It's impossible to admit that now," he said to himself, grimacing with his lips, as if anyone could see this smile of his and be deceived by it. "There's no explanation! Torment, death. . . . Why?"

XI

TWO WEEKS WENT BY LIKE THAT. IN THOSE WEEKS AN event took place that had been desired by Ivan Ilyich and his wife: Petrishchev made a formal proposal. It happened in the evening. The next day Praskovya Fyodorovna went in to her husband, wondering how to announce Fyodor Petrovich's proposal to him, but that very night Ivan Ilyich had taken a turn for the worse. Praskovya Fyodorovna found him on the same sofa, but in a new position. He was lying on his back, groaning and looking ahead with a fixed gaze.

She started talking about medicines. He turned his eyes

to her. She didn't finish what she had begun to say; there was so much anger expressed in those eyes, aimed directly at her.

"For Christ's sake, let me die in peace," he said.

She was about to go, but at that moment his daughter came in and went up to say good morning. He looked at his daughter as he had at his wife and to her questions about his health he drily said to her that he would soon liberate them all from himself. They both said nothing, sat briefly, and went out.

"What can we be blamed for?" Liza said to her mother. "As if we'd done this! I'm sorry for Papa, but why must he torment us?"

The doctor came at the usual time. Ivan Ilyich answered him "yes, no," not taking his angry eyes from him, and finally said:

"You know that you won't be of any help, so leave me."

"We can relieve the suffering," the doctor said.

"You can't do that either; leave me."

The doctor went out into the drawing room and informed Praskovya Fyodorovna that things were very bad and that there was only one resource—opium, to relieve the suffering, which must be terrible.

The doctor said that Ivan Ilyich's physical sufferings were terrible, and that was true; but even more terrible than his physical sufferings were his mental sufferings, and there was his chief torment.

His mental sufferings lay in the fact that that night, as

he looked at Gerasim's sleepy, good-natured face with its high cheekbones, there suddenly had entered his head the thought: *But what if in actual fact all my life, my conscious life, has been "wrong"?*

It occurred to him that the notion that had previously seemed to him a complete impossibility—that he had not lived his life as he should have done—could be the truth. It occurred to him that his barely noticeable attempts at struggling against what was considered good by those in high positions above him, those barely noticeable attempts which he had immediately rejected, could be genuine, and everything else wrong. His work and the structure of his life and his family and his social and professional interests—all that could be wrong. He tried to defend all that to himself. And suddenly he felt the fragility of what he was defending. And there was nothing to defend.

"But if this is so," he said to himself, "and I am leaving life with the realization that I have lost everything I was given and that it's impossible to put right, then what?" He lay on his back and started to go over his whole life afresh. When in the morning he saw the manservant, then his wife, then his daughter, then the doctor—every one of their movements, every one of their words confirmed for him the terrible truth that had been disclosed to him in the night. He saw in them himself, everything by which he had lived, and saw clearly that all this was wrong, all this was a terrible, huge fraud concealing both life and death. This realization increased, increased tenfold his physical sufferings. He groaned and tossed about and pulled at the clothes on him. He felt suffocated and crushed. And he hated them for that.

They gave him a big dose of opium; he lost consciousness, but at dinnertime the same began again. He drove them all away from him and tossed about from side to side.

His wife came to him and said:

"*Jean*, my dear, do this for me. It can't do any harm, but it often helps. So, it's nothing. And people in good health often . . ."

He opened his eyes wide.

"What? Take communion? Why? There's no need to! But then . . ."

She started crying.

"Yes, my dear? I'll call for our man, he's so sweet."

"Fine, very well," he said.

When the priest came and took his confession, he was calmed; he felt a kind of relief from his doubts and, as a consequence of that, from his sufferings, and a moment of hope came to him. He again began to think of his appendix and the possibility of curing it. He received communion with tears in his eyes.

When, after communion, he was put to bed, for a moment he felt comfortable and hope for life appeared again. He began to think of the operation being suggested to him. "To live, I want to live," he said to himself. His wife came to congratulate him on taking communion; she said the usual words and added:

"You feel better, don't you?"

Without looking at her he said, "Yes."

Her clothes, her body, the expression of her face, the sound of her voice—everything said to him one thing: "Wrong. Everything by which you have lived and are living is a lie, a fraud, concealing life and death from you." And as soon as he thought that, hatred rose up in him, and together with hatred agonizing physical suffering, and with those sufferings an awareness of the end, nearby and unavoidable. Something new happened: his breath started to strain and come in spurts and be squeezed out.

His expression when he said "yes" was terrible. Having said that yes, he looked her straight in the eye and with unusual strength for his weakness turned himself facedown and cried:

"Go away, go away, leave me!"

XII

FROM THAT MINUTE BEGAN THREE DAYS OF UNCEASING screams that were so horrible one couldn't hear them from two doors away without feeling horror. The minute he answered his wife, he understood that he was lost, that there was no return, that the end had come, the very end, but the doubt still wasn't resolved; it still remained doubt.

"Oh! Oh! Oh!" he cried out in various tones. He began to

cry out, "I don't want to, no!" and went on like that crying out the letter *O*.[26]

For the whole three days, during which time did not exist for him, he tossed about in the black sack into which he was being pushed by an invisible, insurmountable force. He struggled as a man condemned to death struggles in the arms of the executioner, knowing he cannot save himself; and with every minute he felt that for all his efforts at struggling he was coming nearer and nearer to what filled him with horror. He felt that his agony lay both in being pushed into that black hole and even more in being unable to get into it. He was prevented from climbing in by his declaration that his life had been good. This justification of his life caught on something and stopped him from going forward, and that distressed him most of all.

Suddenly some kind of force struck him in the chest and on the side; his breath was constricted even more; he collapsed into the hole and there at the bottom of the hole some light was showing. There happened to him what he used to experience in a railway carriage when you think you are going forward but are going backward and suddenly realize your true direction.

"Yes, everything was wrong," he said to himself, "but it doesn't matter. I can, I can do what is right. But what is right?" he asked himself, and at once fell silent.

It was the end of the third day, an hour before his death. At that very moment the gymnasium schoolboy quietly slipped into his father's room and approached his bed. The dying man was still crying out despairingly and waving his arms about. One of his hands hit the schoolboy's head. The schoolboy took it, pressed it to his lips, and wept.

At that very moment Ivan Ilyich fell through and saw a light, and it was revealed to him that his life had been wrong but that it was still possible to mend things. He asked himself, "What is right?" and fell silent, listening. Now he felt someone was kissing his hand. He opened his eyes and looked at his son. He felt sorry for him. His wife came to him. He looked at her. She looked at him, mouth open and tears on her nose and cheeks that she hadn't wiped away. He felt sorry for her.

"Yes, I make them unhappy," he thought. "They are sorry for me, but it'll be better for them when I die." He wanted to say that but didn't have the strength to utter it. "However, why say things? One must act," he thought. With a look to his wife he pointed to his son and said:

"Take him away . . . sorry for him . . . and for you . . ." He wanted to add "forgive" but said "give," and not having the strength to correct himself, waved his hand, knowing that He who needed to understand would understand.

And suddenly it became clear to him that what had been oppressing him and not coming to an end—now everything was coming to an end at once, on two sides, on ten sides, on every side. He was sorry for them, he must make it so they had no pain. Free them and free himself from these sufferings. "So good and so simple," he thought. "And the pain?" he asked himself. "Where's it gone? Well, where are you, pain?"

He began to listen.

"There it is. So—let the pain be. And death? Where is it?"

He searched for his old habitual fear of death and didn't find it. Where was death? What death? There was no fear, because there was no death.

Instead of death there was light.

"So that's it!" he suddenly said aloud. "Such joy!"

For him all this took place in a moment, and the significance of this moment didn't change. For those there his death agony lasted two hours more. Something bubbled in his chest; his emaciated body shivered. Then the gurgling and wheezing became less and less frequent.

"It is finished!" someone said above him.

He heard these words and repeated them in his heart. "Death is finished," he said to himself. "It is no more."

He breathed in, stopped halfway, stretched himself, and died.

NOTES

1 the city: in earlier drafts the city was identified as Moscow.

2 requiem service: *panikhida* in Russian. The full requirements of the Russian Orthodox Church are for a *panikhida* to be held on the day of death and then on the third, ninth, and fortieth days after death. This one was presumably on the third day.

3 *vint*: a Russian card game similar to whist and bridge.

4 Privy Councillor: *tayny sovetnik*, the third in the civilian section of the Table of Ranks that governed Russian official life.

5 *le phénix de la famille*: "the star (phoenix) of the family" (French).

6 Sharmer's: a fashionable St. Petersburg tailor.

7 *respice finem*: "look toward the goal" (Latin).

8 Donon's: Donon, one of St. Peterburg's better restaurants, on the Moyka Canal, still in the Baedeker in 1914.

9 *bon enfant*: "a nice boy, one of the lads" (French).

10 *il faut que jeunesse se passe*: "youth must have its fling" (French).

11 *comme il faut*: "proper, gentlemanly" (French).

12 the statutes of 1864: the judicial reform Alexander II instituted in 1864 introduced a completely new court system and a new order of legal proceedings.

13 fifth grade: government service sector of the Table of Ranks. As an examining magistrate Ivan Ilyich would have had the title of state councillor.

14 *de gaieté de coeur*: "out of sheer caprice" (French).

15 Empress Maria's Foundations: the charitable institutions founded by the Empress Maria Alexandrovna (1824–80), wife of Tsar Alexander II.

16 uniform: like all other state servants in imperial Russia, judges wore uniforms.

17 Petrishchev: the son would therefore be Dmitriyevich. Tolstoy slips up; he later becomes Fyodorovich; see n. 23.

18 Jean: the French equivalent of Ivan or John as used by the *comme il faut.*

19 Kiesewetter: Johann Kiesewetter (1766–1819), German philosopher. His textbook on logic, *Grundriss Einer Reinen Allgemeinen Einer Logick*, was published in 1791.

20 Vanya: a diminutive of Ivan by which he would have been known as a child and to his family.

21 *établissement*: "arrangement" (French).

22 Sarah Bernhardt: (1844–1923), world-famous French stage (and early screen) actress and celebrity who toured all of Europe and the Americas. She visited Russia in 1881.

23 Fyodor Petrovich: see n. 17.

24 à la Capoul: in the style of Victor Capoul, a French operatic tenor known for his looks as well as his voice.

25 *Adrienne Lecouvreur*: a French tragic drama (1849) by Eugène Scribe (1791–1861) and Ernest Legouvé (1807–1903). It is based on the life of the eighteenth-century French actress of that name.

26 *O*: in fact, in Russian, *U*, the final letter of "*Ne khochu*"—"I don't want to."

Confession

(Introduction to an Unpublished Work)

I

I WAS CHRISTENED AND BROUGHT UP IN THE ORTHODOX Christian faith. I was instructed in it from my childhood and during the whole time of my boyhood and youth. But when, at the age of eighteen, I left the second year's course of university,[1] I no longer believed anything that I had been taught.

Judging by some of my memories, I never seriously believed but just trusted what I had been taught and what adults professed in front of me; but this trust was very shaky.

I remember that when I was eleven, a boy now long dead, Volodinka M., a pupil at the gymnasium, who came to our house on a Sunday, revealed to us as the very latest thing a discovery made at the gymnasium. The discovery was that there is no God and that everything we had been taught was just lies (this was in 1838). I remember my elder brothers[2] were interested in this piece of news and included me in the discussion. I remember that we all got very excited and saw this information as something very interesting and completely possible.

I also remember that when he was at the university my elder brother Dmitry suddenly took up the faith with the passion characteristic of his nature and started to go to all the church services and to fast and lead a pure and moral life, then all of us, even our elders, kept laughing at him and for some reason nicknamed him Noah. I remember Musin-Pushkin,[3] who was then warden of Kazan University, inviting us to go and dance at his house; he laughingly persuaded my reluctant brother by saying that even David danced before the ark. I shared then the joking attitude of our elders and from it I reached the conclusion that one should learn the catechism and go to church, but not take any of that too seriously. I remember too that I read Voltaire[4] at a very young age and that his witticisms not only didn't shock me but amused me greatly.

My loss of faith happened in me as it happened then and does now among people with our kind of upbringing. In the majority of cases I think it happens like this: people live as all other people do, and they all live on the basis of principles which not only have nothing in common with Christian teaching but also for the most part are in opposition to it; Christian teaching plays no part in life; one never comes across it in one's relations with others and one never has to deal with it in one's own life; this Christian teaching is professed somewhere out there, far from life and independently of it. If you come across it, then it is some external phenomenon that has no connection with life.

Then as now there was no way of learning from a man's life, from his work, whether he was a believer or not. If there is a difference between those who openly profess Orthodoxy and those who deny it, it doesn't favor the former. Then as now the open declaration and profession of Orthodoxy were found for the most part in stupid, cruel, and immoral people who think themselves very important. Intelligence, honesty, uprightness, goodness of heart, and morality were found for the most part in people declaring themselves to be unbelievers.

In schools they teach the catechism and send pupils to church; civil servants are required to provide proof of taking communion. But even now a man from our social circle who has completed his education and isn't in government service could live for decades, and in the old days even longer, without once remembering that he lives among Christians and that he himself is considered to be a member of the Christian Orthodox faith.

So now, just as then, Christian teaching, taken on trust and maintained by outside pressures, gradually dissolves under the influence of knowledge and life experience that are in opposition to it, and a man very often lives for a long time imagining that the Christian teaching given to him as a child is intact within him when it is long gone without a trace.

I was told by S., an intelligent and truthful man, how he stopped believing. He was already aged twenty-six and once, staying somewhere for the night while out hunting, he began to say his prayers out of old childhood habit. His elder brother, who was hunting with him, lay on the hay and watched him. When S. had finished and started to go to bed, his brother said to him, "Are you still doing that?" And they said nothing more to each other. And from that day on S. stopped saying his prayers and going to church. And it's now been thirty years that he hasn't prayed or taken communion or gone to church. And not because he knew his brother's convictions and began to share them, not because he had reached some decision in his heart, but only because those words spoken by his brother were like the tap of a finger on a wall ready to fall under its own weight; those words were an indicator that where he thought faith existed there had long been a void, and that therefore the words he spoke and the signs of the cross and the bows he made when he stood in prayer were all completely meaningless actions. Having recognized their meaninglessness he could not continue them.

That was the case and still is, I think, with the great majority of people. I am talking about people with our kind of education; I am talking about people who are truthful with themselves, but not about those who make the very fact of faith a means of attaining some ephemeral goals. (These people are the most fundamental unbelievers, because if faith for them is a means of attaining some worldly goals, then that is certainly not faith.) People with our kind of education are in a position where the light of knowledge and life have dissolved artificial knowledge, and either they have noticed this and emptied that space or they haven't yet noticed it.

The Christian teaching given to me in childhood disappeared in me as in others, only with the difference that as I began to read a great deal and to think very early on, so my rejection of Christian teaching became a conscious one very early on. From the age of sixteen I stopped saying my prayers and of my own volition stopped going to church and fasting. I stopped believing in all that had been given to me since childhood, but I did believe in something. What I did believe in I couldn't possibly have said. I did believe in God or rather did not deny God, but I couldn't have said what kind of god; I didn't deny Christ and his teaching, but I also couldn't have said where his teaching lay.

Now, remembering that time, I see clearly that my faith—the thing that guided my life, apart from animal instincts—my only real faith at that time was a faith in self-perfection. But I couldn't have said in what that self-perfection lay and what its goal was. I tried to improve myself mentally—I studied everything I could and everything life thrust in front of me; I perfected myself physically, developing strength and agility by all kinds of exercise and training myself by all kinds of deprivations in endurance and staying power. And I thought of all that as self-perfection. The beginning of all this of course was moral self-perfection, but that was soon replaced by self-perfection in general, that is, the desire to be better not in my own eyes or the eyes of God but the desire to be better in the eyes of other people. And very soon this urge to be better in the eyes of other people was replaced by the desire to be more powerful than other people, that is, more famous, more important, richer than others.

II

ONE DAY I'LL TELL THE STORY OF MY LIFE—BOTH A touching and an instructive one for those ten years of my youth. I think that many, many people have experienced the same. I wanted to be good with all my soul, but I was young, I had passions, and I was alone, completely alone, when I was seeking good. Every time I tried to show what made up my innermost desires, to show that I wanted to be morally good, I met with scorn and mockery; but as soon as I abandoned myself to vile passions, I was praised and encouraged. Ambition, love of power, avarice, lust, pride, anger, revenge—all these had respect. Giving myself over to these passions, I became like a grown man and I felt that people were pleased with me. My kind aunt, the purest of beings, with whom I lived, always used to tell me that there was nothing she wished for me more than that I should have a liaison with a married woman: "*Rien ne forme un jeune homme comme une liaison avec une femme comme il faut*";[5] there was another happiness she wanted for me—to be an aide-de-camp, and best of all to the emperor; and the supreme happiness, that I should marry a very rich girl and as the result of this marriage have as many serfs as possible.

I cannot remember these years without horror, revulsion, and pain in my heart. I killed people in war, I challenged people to duels in order to kill them, I lost at cards, I consumed the labor of peasants, I punished them, I fornicated, I deceived. Lies, theft, adultery of every kind, drunkenness, violence, murder. . . . There was no crime I did not commit, and for all this my contemporaries praised me and thought me a relatively moral man, as they still do.

I lived like that for about ten years.

At this time I began to write, out of vanity, greed, and pride. In my writing I did the same as in life. To have the fame and the money for which I was writing I had to conceal the good and display the bad. So I did. How many times under the pretense of indifference and even of slight mockery did I contrive to conceal my aspirations to good, which constituted the meaning of my life? And I achieved my aim: I was praised.

I came to Petersburg at the age of twenty-six after the war[6] and met writers. They accepted me like one of their own and flattered me, and before I had time to look around I had adopted the writer's professional views on life held by those whom I met, and these completely destroyed in me all my former attempts to become better. Faced with the dissoluteness of my life, these views provided a theory that justified it.

The view of life held by these people, my comrades in writing, consisted of this: life in general moves on by development, and the main part in this development is played by us, people who think, and the main influence among people who think is held by us—artists, poets. Our vocation is to teach people. To avoid the natural question being put to one—what do I know and what can I teach?—the theory made it clear that one didn't have to know anything except that the artist and poet teach unconsciously. I was thought to be a marvelous artist and poet, and so it was very natural for me to adopt this theory. As an artist, a poet, I wrote, I taught myself without knowing what. I was paid money for that; I had fine food, a house, women, society; I had fame. So it had to be that what I taught was very good.

This belief in the meaning of poetry and the development of life was a religious faith, and I was one of its priests. To be its priest was very profitable and agreeable. And for quite a long time I lived in this faith without doubting its truth. But in the second and especially the third year of this life I began to have doubts in the infallibility of this faith and began to investigate it. The first occasion for doubt was when I started to notice that the priests of this faith didn't always agree among themselves. Some said, "We are the best and most useful teachers; we teach what is necessary, but others teach wrongly." But others said, "No, we are the true teachers but you are teaching wrongly." And they argued, quarreled, cursed, deceived, cheated one another. Furthermore, there were many people among us who were didn't care about who was right and who was not right but were simply after attaining their mercenary aims with the help of our activity. All this made me doubt the truth of our faith.

Furthermore, having had doubts about the truth of the actual writers' faith, I started to observe its priests more attentively and came to the conclusion that almost all of the priests of this faith, the writers, were immoral and mostly bad people, worthless in character—much lower than the people I had encountered in my previous debauched and military life—but self-confident and pleased with themselves as only truly saintly people can be, or else those who do not know what sanctity is. These people disgusted me; I disgusted myself and I understood that this faith was a fraud.

But it's strange that although I soon understood the falsehood of this faith and renounced it, I did not renounce the position these people had given me—the position of an artist, poet, teacher. I naively imagined that I was a poet and artist, and that I could teach everyone without knowing myself what I was teaching. That is what I did.

From my association with these people I took away a new vice—a morbidly developed pride and crazy certainty that I was called to teach people without myself knowing what I was teaching.

Now when I remember that time and my state of mind then and the state of mind of such people (of whom there are by the way many thousands), I feel it's pitiful and frightening and absurd—there comes just the feeling you get in a madhouse.

We were all convinced then that we had to talk and talk, write, and publish—as quickly as possible, as much as possible, that all this was necessary for the good of mankind. And thousands of us, contradicting and abusing each other, kept publishing and writing while we taught others. And without noticing that we knew nothing, that we didn't know how to answer the simplest questions of life—what is good; what is bad?—we all without listening to each other spoke at once, sometimes indulging each other and praising each other, so that I too was indulged and praised; sometimes getting angry and shouting each other down, just like in a madhouse.

Thousands of workmen worked to the limits of their strength day and night, setting type and printing millions of words, and the mail took them all over Russia, and we kept teaching, teaching, teaching more and more and never were able to finish teaching everything and kept getting angry that we weren't listened to very much.

All horribly strange, but now I understand it. Our real heartfelt reasoning was that we wanted to get as much money and praise as we could. To achieve that aim we could do nothing else but write books and newspapers. So we did that. But in order for us to do such useless work and have the certainty that we were very important people, we needed another piece of reasoning that would justify our activity.

And so we thought up the following: everything that exists is reasonable. Everything that exists goes on developing. It goes on developing through education. Education is measured by the dissemination of books and newspapers. And we are paid money and respected because we write books and newspapers, and so we are very useful and good people. This reasoning would have been very good if we had all agreed; but since for every thought pronounced by one there always appeared a thought, diametrically opposite, pronounced by another, that should have made us think again. But we didn't notice that. We were paid money, and people of our persuasion praised us—so we, each one of us, thought ourselves right.

It is now clear to me that this was no different than a madhouse; I only dimly suspected this then and simply, like all madmen, called everyone mad but myself.

III

I LIVED LIKE THIS, GIVEN OVER TO THIS MADNESS, FOR six years more until my marriage. During this time I traveled abroad. Life in Europe and meeting Europe's prominent people and scholars confirmed me even more in that belief in general self-perfection by which I lived, because I found that same belief in them too. This belief took in me the usual form it has in the majority of educated people of our time. This belief was expressed by the word "progress." I thought then that this word did express something. I didn't yet understand that, tormented like every living man by questions of "How can I live better?," in answering, "Live in conformity with progress," I was saying exactly what a man, carried along in a boat by the waves and the wind, will say to the captain when the only question facing him is "Where should I steer for?" if he says without answering the question, "We are being carried along somewhere."

I didn't see that then. Only from time to time not my reason but my feelings revolted against this generally prevalent superstition with which people conceal their lack of understanding of life in our time. Thus during my stay in Paris the sight of an execution disclosed to me the shaky foundations of my superstitious belief in progress. When I saw the head parted from the body and both head and body separately falling noisily into the bin, then I understood—not with my mind but with my whole being—that no theories of the rationality of existence and progress could justify this act, and if all the people of the world, from the world's creation, according to whatever theories, were to find that this is necessary—I knew that it was not necessary, that it was bad, and that therefore the judge of what is good and necessary is not what people say and do, but I myself and my heart. Another occasion of the inadequacy of the superstition of progress was the death of my brother.[7] A clever, kind, serious man, he fell ill while still young, suffered for more than a year, and died in agony, without understanding why he had lived and understanding still less why he was dying. No theories could give any answer to these questions either for me or for him during the time of his slow and agonizing dying.

But these were only infrequent occasions of doubt; in reality I continued to live only professing my belief in progress. "Everything is evolving and I am evolving, and why I am evolving together with everyone else will be made clear." That was how I then had to formulate my faith.

Returning from abroad, I settled in the country and became occupied with peasant schools.[8] This occupation was particularly to my liking because it contained none of those lies now obvious to me that had already so struck me in the business of literary education. Here too I was acting in the name of progress, but by now I was treating progress itself critically. I told myself that progress in some of its manifestations was carried out wrongly and that here I had to treat primitive people, peasant children, quite freely, offering them a choice of the path of progress that they wanted.

In reality I kept circling around one insoluble problem—to teach without knowing what. In the higher spheres of literary activity it was clear to me that I should not teach without knowing what, because I saw that all of them taught different things and only concealed their ignorance from one another by disputes; here, with the peasant children, I thought that I could get around this difficulty by letting the children study what they wanted. Now I find it ridiculous remembering how I prevaricated in trying to carry out my whim of teaching, although I knew very well in the depths of my heart that I could teach nothing of what should be taught, because I myself did not know what should be taught. After a year spent in school activities, I went abroad a second time to learn there how I could manage to be able to teach others while knowing nothing myself.

And I thought I had learned this abroad and, armed with this great wisdom, I returned to Russia in the year of the emancipation of the peasants[9] and, taking up the post of arbitrator,[10] I started teaching the uneducated folk in schools and the educated in a journal I began to publish. The business seemed to go well, but I felt that I wasn't altogether healthy mentally and that this couldn't go on for a long time. And then perhaps I would have come to that despair I came to at the age of fifty if I hadn't had another side of life that I hadn't yet experienced and which promised me salvation: that was family life.

For the course of a year I worked with arbitration, the schools, and the journal and I became so exhausted, in particular from my confusion, and so burdensome did I find the struggle over arbitration, so muddled seemed my school activity, so hateful my prevarications in the journal, which always came from one and the same thing—my desire to teach everyone and conceal the fact that I didn't know what to teach—that I became ill, more in mind that body, abandoned everything, and went off into the steppe to the Bashkirs to breathe air, drink *koumiss*[11] and lead a simple life.

Returning from there, I married. The new conditions of a happy family life now completely diverted me from my search for the general meaning of life. During this time my life was focused on the family, on my wife, on my children, and so on trying to increase my livelihood. My personal aspiration for self-perfection, which had already been replaced by an aspiration to perfection generally, to progress, was now directly replaced by an aspiration to the best possible life for myself and my family.

So fifteen more years went by.

In spite of the fact that during those fifteen years I considered writing to be nonsense, I still went on writing. I had already tasted the temptation of writing, the temptation of huge monetary reward and applause for worthless work, and I gave myself up to it as a means to better my material position and suppress in my soul all questions about the meaning of my own life and of life in general.

I wrote, teaching what for me was the only truth: that one should live so that life for oneself and one's family was the best possible.

So I lived, but five years ago something very strange started to happen to me: there started to come over me moments at first of bewilderment, of life stopping as if I didn't know how to live or what to do, and I became lost and fell into despair. But this passed and I went on living as before. Then these moments of bewilderment began to be repeated more and more frequently and always in the same form. These moments of life coming to a halt were always expressed in the very same questions: Why? Well, and then what?

At first I thought that these were just pointless, irrelevant questions. I thought all this was known and that if and when I wanted to take up finding the answers, it wouldn't be much work for me—it was only that now I didn't have the time to do that, but when I turned my mind to it, I would find the answers. But the questions began to be repeated more and more frequently; answers were demanded more and more insistently; and like spots of ink that keep falling into one place, all these questions without answers merged into a single black stain.

There happened what happens to everyone who falls ill with a mortal internal disease. At first there appear some insignificant symptoms of indisposition to which the sick man pays no attention, then these symptoms recur more and more often and merge into one continuous suffering. The suffering grows and before the sick man has time to look around, he recognizes that what he took for exhaustion is the thing that is for him more important than anything in the world—that it's death.

That happened to me too. I understood that this was no casual exhaustion but something very important, and that if these same questions kept on being repeated, then one must answer them. And I tried to answer. The questions seemed such stupid, simple, childish questions. But as soon as I tackled them and tried to find the answers, I at once became certain first that these were not childish and stupid questions but the most important and profound questions in life, and second that I could not, just could not answer them, however much I thought about it. Before occupying myself with the Samara estate,[12] the education of my son, the writing of a book, I had to know why I would be doing that. As long as I didn't know why, I couldn't do anything. As I thought about estate management, which engaged me a lot at that time, there would suddenly come into my head the question: "Very well, you'll have sixteen thousand acres in the province of Samara, and three hundred horses, and then what?" I was completely thrown and didn't know what more to think. Or starting to think about how I was educating my children, I would say to myself, "Why?" Or considering how the welfare of the people might be achieved, I suddenly would say to myself, "But what's it to do with me?" Or thinking about the fame my works would bring me, I would say to myself, "Very well, you'll be more famous than Gogol, Pushkin, Shakespeare, Molière, than all the writers in the world—so what?"

And I couldn't answer anything, anything at all.

IV

MY LIFE CAME TO A HALT. I COULD BREATHE, EAT, drink, sleep, and I couldn't *not* breathe, eat, drink, sleep; but I had no life because I had no desires in the fulfillment of which I might find any meaning. If I desired something, then I knew in advance that whether I fulfilled my desire or not, nothing would come of it.

If an enchantress had come and offered to fulfill my desires for me, I wouldn't have known what to say. If in drunken moments I did have not so much desires as the habits of old desires, then in sober moments I knew that it was delusion, that there was nothing to desire. I could not even desire to learn the truth because I guessed wherein it lay. The truth was that life is nonsense.

I sort of lived a life and went along and approached the precipice and clearly saw that there was nothing ahead but doom. And I couldn't stop and I couldn't go back and I couldn't close my eyes so as not to see that there was nothing ahead but the delusion of life and happiness and real suffering and real death—complete annihilation.

Life became hateful to me—an insuperable force pulled me toward somehow ridding myself of it. I cannot say that I wanted to kill myself. The force that pulled me away from life was stronger, more ample, more generalized than wishing. It was a force like the earlier urge toward life, only in the opposite direction. I walked away from life with all my might. The thought of suicide came to me as naturally as once there had come thoughts of the perfection of life. This thought was so tempting that I had to use tricks against myself in order not to carry it out too hastily. I didn't want to hurry only because I wanted to make every effort to sort things out. I said to myself, if I don't sort things out now I'll always have time. And so then I, a happy man, removed a cord from my room where I was alone every evening as I undressed in order not to hang myself from the beam between the cupboards; and I stopped going out hunting with my gun so as not to be too tempted by an easy way of ridding myself of life. I didn't know myself what I wanted: I was afraid of life; I rushed away from it and at the same time I still hoped for something from it.

And this happened to me at a time when on every side I had what is considered to be perfect happiness: it was when I wasn't yet fifty. I had a kind, loving, and loved wife; good children; and a large estate which without labor on my part grew and increased. I was respected by family and friends, was praised more than ever before by the world at large, and without especial self-deception could consider myself to have fame. Moreover, I not only wasn't sickly physically or spiritually but on the contrary had both spiritual and physical strength such as I seldom encountered in my contemporaries: physically I could mow the hay and keep up with the peasants; mentally I could work for eight or ten hours at a stretch without feeling any consequences from the effort. And in this situation I came to such a state that I couldn't live, and being frightened of death, I had to be cunning with myself so as not to take my life.

This mental state expressed itself for me as follows: My life was some kind of stupid and wicked joke played on me. In spite of the fact that I did not acknowledge any "somebody" who created me, this idea that somebody had wickedly and stupidly played a trick on me by bringing me into the world was to me the most natural idea.

Involuntarily I imagined that somewhere out there was somebody who, looking at me now, was laughing at how I had lived for a whole thirty or forty years, studying, developing, growing in body and spirit, and how now, having reached the peak of life, from which it all lay open, I stood on that peak like a complete fool, clearly understanding that there was nothing at all in life, that there hasn't been and there won't be. "And he finds it funny . . ."

But whether there is or isn't this somebody who was laughing at me gave me no relief. I couldn't attribute any intelligent meaning to a single act or to the whole of my life. I was surprised that I couldn't understand that at the very beginning. All this had been known to everyone for so long. One day sickness and death will come (and have come) to my loved ones, to myself, and nothing will remain but stink and worms. My works, of whatever kind, will all be forgotten sooner or later, and I too will not exist. So why worry? How can a man see this and go on living—that is what's astonishing. You can only live as long as you're drunk with life; but when you sober up, you can't help but see that all this is just a fraud, and a stupid fraud. Precisely that: there's nothing even amusing or witty about it; it's simply cruel and stupid.

Long ago there was told an oriental fable about a traveler caught in the steppe by a raging wild beast. To escape from the beast the traveler jumps into an empty well, but at the bottom of the well he sees a dragon opening its jaws wide to devour him. And the wretched man, not daring to climb out so as not to be killed by the raging beast, not daring either to jump to the bottom of the well so as not to be devoured by the dragon, grasps the branches of a wild shrub growing in the crevices of the well and holds on to it. His arms grow weak and he feels that he will soon have to give in to the doom that awaits him on both sides; but he keeps hanging on, and while he hangs on, he looks around and sees two mice, one black, the other white, regularly going around the trunk of the shrub from which he is hanging and gnawing it. Any moment the shrub will snap of its own accord and tear itself free and he will fall into the jaws of the dragon. The traveler sees this and knows that he will inevitably perish, but while he is hanging he searches around him and finds drops of honey on the leaves of the shrub; he reaches for them with his tongue and licks them. So do I hang on to the branches of life, knowing that the dragon of death is ineluctably waiting, ready to tear me to pieces, and I cannot understand why I entered this torment. And I try to suck the honey which once used to comfort me; but this honey no longer gladdens me, and the white and black mice—day and night—gnaw away at the branch onto which I am holding. I can see the dragon clearly and the honey is no longer sweet for me. I can only see two things—the inescapable dragon and the mice—and I can't turn my eyes from them. And this is not a fable but the honest, undisputable truth that all can understand.

The former illusion of the joys of life, which used to suppress the horror of the dragon, deceives me no more. Only do not tell me, "You can't understand the meaning of life; don't think, live"—I can't do that because I did it for too long before. Now I can't help seeing day and night running along and leading me to death. I see only this because only this is the truth. All the rest is lies.

Those two drops of honey which used to take my eyes away from the cruel truth longer than the others—my love for the family and for writing which I called art—are sweet for me no more.

"The family . . . ," I said to myself, but the family is my wife and children; they too are people. They are in the very same conditions as I am; they must either live in a lie or see the terrible truth. Why should they live? Why should I love them, guard them, nurture and watch over them? For them to reach the despair that is in me, or for their minds to be numbed! Loving them I can't conceal the truth from them—each step forward in knowledge leads them to that truth. And the truth is death.

Art, poetry? For a long time, influenced by the success of popular adulation, I convinced myself that this was work I could do, in spite of the fact that death would come, which would destroy everything—me and my works and the memory of them; but I soon saw that they too were an illusion. It was clear to me that art was a decoration of life, an enticement to life. But life has lost its enticement for me; how can I entice others? While I was living a life that was not my own but an alien life was bearing me along on its waves, while I believed that life had a meaning although I couldn't express it, all kinds of reflections of life, in poetry and art, gave me joy; I was happy looking at life in art's little mirror, but when I began to look for the meaning of life, when I felt the necessity of living myself, that little mirror became for me unnecessary, superfluous, and ridiculous, or painful. I could no longer comfort myself with the fact that I saw in the mirror that my situation was stupid and desperate. It was all very well for me to enjoy that when I believed in the depth of my soul that my life has a meaning. Then the play of light and shade—of the comic, tragic, moving, beautiful, terrible in life—entertained me. But when I knew that life is meaningless and terrible, the game in the mirror could no longer amuse me. No sweetness of honey could be sweet for me when I saw the dragon and the mice gnawing away at my support.

But that's not all. If I had simply understood that life has no meaning, I might have known that calmly, could have known that this was my fate. But I couldn't be content with that. If I had been like a man in a forest from which he knows there is no way out, I could have lived; but I was like a man lost in a forest who has been overcome by terror through being lost, and he rushes to and fro trying to find the road; he knows that every step makes him more lost, and he can't stop rushing about.

Now this was horrible. And in order to escape this horror I wanted to kill myself. I felt horror before what awaited me—I knew that this horror was more horrible than my situation itself, but I couldn't banish it and I couldn't patiently wait for the end. However convincing the realization that inevitably a vessel in the heart would burst or something would crack and all would be over, I could not patiently wait for the end. The horror of the darkness was too great and I wanted to be freed of it, quickly, quickly, by a noose or a bullet. And it was this feeling more strongly than anything else that led me toward suicide.

V

"BUT MAYBE I HAVE OVERLOOKED SOMETHING, HAVEN'T understood something," I said to myself several times. "It cannot be that this state of despair is natural to human beings." And I searched for explanations of my questions in all the branches of knowledge that human beings have acquired. And I searched long and agonizingly and not just out of idle curiosity; I didn't search limply but I searched agonizingly, persistently, day and night; I searched as a dying man searches for salvation, and I found nothing.

I searched in all the sciences and not only did I find nothing but I became convinced that all those who had searched in knowledge as I had likewise had found nothing. And not only had they found nothing but they plainly admitted that the very thing which brought me to despair, the meaninglessness of life, is the only unquestionable knowledge open to man.

I searched everywhere, and thanks to a life spent in study—but also to the fact that, through my connections with the world of learning, I had access to the actual scholars in all the various branches of knowledge who were ready to disclose to me all they knew not just in books but in talking to me—I learned all that knowledge offers in answer to the question of life.

For a long time I could not believe that knowledge gives no answer to the questions of life apart from the one it does give. For a long time as I looked at the portentousness and serious tone of science as it asserts its arguments, which have nothing in common with the questions of human life, I thought I was failing to understand something. For a long time I felt intimidated in front of knowledge and I thought that the incompatibility of its answers to my questions came through no fault of knowledge but from my ignorance; but this for me was no joke, no game, but the matter of my whole life, and willy-nilly I was drawn to the conclusion that my questions were the only legitimate questions serving as the basis for any kind of knowledge, and that it wasn't I who was at fault with my questions but science if it makes claims to answer these questions.

My question, which at the age of fifty brought me to the point of suicide, was the very simple question that lies in the soul of every human being, from a silly child to the wisest sage—the question without which life is impossible, as I experienced in actual fact. The question is this: What will come from what I do and from what I will do tomorrow—what will come from my whole life?

Expressed differently, the question would be this: Why should I live, why should I wish for anything, why should I do anything? One can put the question differently again: Is there any meaning in my life that wouldn't be destroyed by the death that inevitably awaits me?

I looked for an answer to this question in human knowledge, a question expressed in different ways but remaining one and the same. And I found in their attitude to this question all human sciences divided, as it were, into two opposite hemispheres at the opposite ends of which are two poles, one negative, the other positive, but at neither pole any answers to the questions of life.

One range of sciences seems not to recognize the question, though it clearly and precisely answers its own independently put questions: that is the range of experimental sciences, with mathematics at their extreme point. The other range of sciences recognizes the question but doesn't answer it: this is the range of speculative sciences, with metaphysics at their extreme point.

From my earliest youth I was interested in speculative science but later I was attracted by the mathematical and natural sciences, and until I had clearly put my question to myself, until this question had grown within me, insistently demanding an answer, I was satisfied by those imitations of answers to the question that knowledge gives.

Sometimes in the experimental sphere I said to myself, "Everything develops, is differentiated, moves toward complexity and perfection, and there are laws that govern this movement. You are a part of the whole. Having learned the whole, insofar as that is possible, and having learned the law of development, you will learn both your place in that whole and your own self." I'm ashamed to admit it, but there was a time when I was apparently satisfied by this. It was that very time when I myself was developing and becoming more complex. My muscles grew and strengthened, my memory was enriched, my capacity for thought and understanding became greater, I grew and developed, and as I felt that growth in myself it was natural for me to think that this was indeed the law of the whole world, in which I would also find the answer to the question of my life. But there came a time when growth stopped in me—I felt I was not developing but drying up, my muscles becoming weaker, my teeth falling out—and I saw that not only did this law explain nothing to me but that such a law had never existed and could not exist, and that I just took for a law what I found in my own self at a particular time of my life. I took a stricter view of the definition of this law, and it became clear to me that there could not be laws of infinite development; it became clear that to say, "In infinite space and time everything develops, becomes more perfect, more complex, is differentiated" means to say nothing. All of these are words without meaning, because in infinity there is neither complex nor simple, neither front nor back, neither better nor worse.

The main thing was that my personal question—what exactly am I with my desires—remained completely without an answer. And I understood that all of these sciences were very interesting, very attractive, but that they are precise and clear in inverse proportion to their application to the questions of life; the less they are applicable to the questions of life, the more precise and clear they are; the more they attempt to give solutions to the questions of life, the more unclear and unattractive they become. If you turn to a branch of those sciences that try to give a solution to the questions of life—to physiology, psychology, biology, sociology—there you will find an astounding poverty of thought, a very great lack of clarity, completely unjustified claims to answer questions that lie outside their subject and neverending contradictions between one thinker and others, and even within himself. If you turn to a branch of the sciences that is not concerned with solving the questions of life but answers its own scientific, specialized questions, then you are captivated by the power of human intellect but you know in advance that there are no answers to the questions of life. These sciences directly ignore the questions of life. They say, "We have no answers to 'What are you?' and 'Why do you live?' and are not concerned with this; but if you need to know the laws of light, of chemical compounds, the laws of the development of organisms, if you need to know the laws of bodies and their forms and the relation of numbers and quantities, if you need to know the laws of your own mind, to all that we have clear, precise, and unquestionable answers."

In general the relation of the experimental sciences to the question of life can be expressed thus. Question: Why do I live? Answer: In infinite space, in infinite time, infinitely small particles change in infinite complexity, and when you understand the laws of these changes, then you will understand why you live.

Then in the speculative sphere I said to myself, "All of mankind lives and develops on the basis of the spiritual principles, the *ideals*, that guide it. These ideals are expressed in religions, in sciences, art, forms of government. These ideals become higher and higher, and mankind is going toward the highest good. I am a part of mankind, and therefore my vocation is to further the awareness and the fulfillment of mankind's ideals." And at the time of my feeblemindedness I was satisfied by this, but as soon as the question of life put itself clearly within me, this whole theory collapsed at once. Without mentioning the unscrupulous imprecision with which the sciences of this kind present conclusions drawn from studying a small part of mankind as general conclusions, without mentioning the mutual contradictions among various advocates of this theory of the nature of mankind's ideals, the strangeness, not to say the stupidity, of this theory lies in the fact that in order to answer the questions confronting every man—"What am I?" or "What should I do?"—a man must first of all answer the question, "What is the life of all of mankind that is unknown to me, of which I know only a minute part over a minute period of time?" To understand what he is, a man must first of all understand the whole of mysterious humanity made up of people just like himself who don't understand themselves.

I must admit that there was a time when I did believe this. That was the time when I had my favorite ideals that justified my random desires, and I tried to develop a theory by which I could look at those random desires as a law of mankind. But as soon as the question of life put itself within my spirit in all its clarity, this answer at once dissolved in dust. And I understood that just as among the experimental sciences there are true sciences and semi-sciences that attempt to give answers to questions outside their concern, so I understood that in this sphere too there is a whole range of the most widespread branches of knowledge trying to answer questions outside their concern. The semi-sciences in this sphere—jurisprudence, the social and historical sciences—attempt to answer man's questions by each falsely and in its own way answering the question of life of all mankind.

But just as in the sphere of the experimental sciences a man sincerely asking, "How should I live?" cannot be satisfied with the answer, "Study the infinite changes of infinite particles in infinite space, changes infinite in time and in complexity, and then you will understand your life," so a sincere man cannot be satisfied by the answer, "Study the life of all mankind of which we know neither beginning nor end, and of which we don't know even a small part, and then you will understand your life." And in just the same way as in the experimental semi-sciences, these semi-sciences too fill up with obscurities, imprecisions, stupidities, and contradictions the further they deviate from their subjects. The subject of experimental science is the causal sequence of material phenomena. Experimental science has only to introduce the question of a final cause and the result is nonsense. The subject of speculative science is awareness of the essence of life that has no cause. Introduce the study of causal phenomena—like social and historical phenomena—and the result is nonsense.

Experimental science only produces positive knowledge and displays the greatness of the human mind when it doesn't introduce a final cause into its studies. And speculative science on the contrary is only a science and displays the greatness of the human mind when it completely sets aside questions about a sequence of causal phenomena and considers man only in relation to a final cause. Such in this area is the science that constitutes the pole of this hemisphere—metaphysics, or speculative philosophy. This science clearly asks the questions, "What am I and what is the whole world? And why do I exist and why does the whole world exist?" And ever since it has existed it has given an identical answer. Whether a philosopher calls the essence of life, which is in me and in everything that exists, ideas or substance or spirit or will, the philosopher says one single thing: that this essence exists and that I am this essence, but he doesn't know why it exists, and if he is a precise thinker he gives no answer. I ask, "Why should this essence of life exist? What will come of its existence now and in the future?" And philosophy not only doesn't answer but all it does is ask that question. And if it is true philosophy, then all its work lies solely in asking this question clearly. And if it keeps firmly to its subject, then to the question, "What am I and what is the whole world?" it can give no other answer but "Everything and nothing"; and to the question, "Why does the world exist and why do I exist?" just the answer "I don't know."

So however I may examine philosophy's speculative replies, in no way will I receive anything resembling an answer—and not because, as in the clear area of experimental science, the answer isn't related to my question, but because here, although all the theoretical work is directed precisely toward my question, there is no answer, and instead of an answer one gets the same question, only in a more complicated form.

VI

IN MY SEARCH FOR ANSWERS TO THE QUESTION OF LIFE I had exactly the same feeling as a man who has lost his way in a forest.

He has come out into a clearing, climbed a tree, and has a clear view of limitless space, but he sees that there is no house there and that there cannot be one; he goes into the trees, into the darkness, and sees darkness, and there too there is no house.

In the same way I wandered in this forest of human knowledge between the rays of light of the mathematical and experimental sciences, which opened up clear horizons to me but in a direction where there could be no house, and into the darkness of the speculative sciences, where I was plunged into greater darkness the further I moved on, and finally I was convinced that there was not and could not be any way out.

As I gave myself up to the brighter side of the sciences, I understood that I was only taking my eyes off the question. However enticing and clear the horizons opening upon before me, however enticing it was to plunge myself into the infinity of these sciences, I already understood that the clearer these sciences were, the less they served me, the less they answered my question.

"Well, I know," I said to myself, "everything that science so insistently wants to know, but on this path there is no answer to the question of the meaning of my life." In the speculative sphere I understood that although, or precisely because, science's aim was directed straight at the answer to my question, there was no other answer than the one I was giving myself: "What is the meaning of my life?" "None." Or: "What will come out of my life?" "Nothing." Or: "Why does everything exist that exists, and why do I exist?" "Because it exists."

Asking questions on one side of human science, I received a countless quantity of precise answers to questions I wasn't asking: about the chemical composition of the stars; the movement of the sun toward the constellation Hercules; the origin of species and of man; the forms of infinitely small atoms; the vibration of infinitely small, weightless particles of ether—but there was only one answer in this area of science to my question, "In what is the meaning of my life?": "You are what you call your life; you are an ephemeral, casual connection of particles. The interaction, the change of these particles produces in you what you call your life. This connection will last some time; then the interaction of these particles will stop—and what you call your life will stop and all your questions will stop too. You are a lump of something stuck together by chance. The lump decays. The lump calls this decay its life. The lump will disintegrate and the decay and all its questions will come to an end." That is the answer given by the bright side of science, and it cannot give any other if it just strictly follows its principles.

With such an answer it turns out that the answer doesn't answer the question. I need to know the meaning of my life, but its being a particle of the infinite not only gives it no meaning but destroys any possible meaning.

The vague compromises that this side of precise experimental science makes with speculative science, in which it is stated that the meaning of life lies in development and furthering that development, by their imprecision and vagueness cannot be classed as answers.

The other side of science, the speculative, when it strictly adheres to its principles in answering the question directly, gives and has given the same answer everywhere and in all ages: "The world is something infinite and unintelligible. Human life is an incomprehensible piece of this incomprehensible 'whole'." Again I exclude all the compromises between speculative and experimental science that constitute the whole ballast of the semi-sciences, the so-called jurisprudential, political, and historical. Into these sciences again one finds wrongly introduced the notions of development, of perfection, with the difference only that there it was the development of the whole whereas here it is of the life of people. What is wrong is the same: development and perfection in the infinite can have neither aim nor direction and in relation to my question give no answer.

Where speculative science is exact, namely in true philosophy—not in what Schopenhauer[13] called "professorial philosophy" which only serves to distribute all existing phenomena in neat philosophical tables and give them new names—there where a philosopher doesn't lose sight of the essential question, the answer, always one and the same, is the answer given by Socrates,[14] Solomon, Buddha.

"We will come near truth only inasmuch as we depart from life," said Socrates, preparing for death. "What do we who love truth strive for in life? To be freed of the body and of all the evil that comes from the life of the body. If that is so, then how should we not rejoice when death comes to us?

"A wise man seeks death his whole life and therefore death holds no fear for him."

Schopenhauer says: "We have recognized the inmost nature of the world as will, and all its phenomena as only the objectivity of will; and we have followed this objectivity from the unconscious working of obscure forces of Nature up to the completely conscious action of man. Therefore we shall by no means evade the consequence, that with the free denial, the surrender of the will, all those phenomena are also abolished; that constant strain and effort without end and without rest at all the grades of objectivity, in which and through which the world consists; the multifarious forms succeeding each other in gradation; the whole manifestation of the will; and, finally, also the universal forms of this manifestation, time and space, and also its last fundamental form, subject and object; all are abolished. No will; no idea; no world.

"Before us there is certainly only nothingness. But that which resists this passing into nothing, our nature, is indeed just the will to live (*Wille zum Leben*), which we ourselves are as it is our world. That we abhor annihilation so greatly is simply another expression of the fact that we so strenuously will life, and are nothing but this will, and know nothing besides it. . . . What remains after the entire abolition of will is for all those who are still full of will certainly nothing; but, conversely, to those in whom the will has turned and has denied itself, this our world, which is so real, with all its suns and Milky Ways—is nothing."[15]

"Vanity of vanities," says Solomon, "vanity of vanities; all is vanity. What profit hath a man of all his labor which he taketh under the sun? One generation passeth away, and another generation cometh: but the earth abideth for ever.

. . . The thing that hath been, it is that that shall be; and that which is done is that which shall be done: and there is no new thing under the sun. Is there anything whereof it may be said, See, this is new? It hath been already of old time, which was before us. There is no remembrance of former things; neither shall there be any remembrance of things that are to come with those that shall come after. I Ecclesiastes was king over Israel in Jerusalem. And I gave my heart to seek and search out by wisdom concerning all things that are done under heaven: this sore travail hath God given to the sons of man to be exercised therewith. I have seen all the works that are done under the sun; and behold all is vanity and vexation of spirit. . . . I communed with mine own heart saying, Lo, I am come to great estate, and have gotten more wisdom than all they that have been before me in Jerusalem: yea, my heart had great experience of wisdom and knowledge. And I gave my heart to know wisdom, and to know madness and folly: I perceived that this also is vexation of spirit. For in much wisdom is much grief: and he that increaseth knowledge increaseth sorrow.

"I said in mine heart, Go to now, I will prove thee with mirth and will rejoice in good deeds: and, behold, this also is vanity. I said of laughter, It is mad: and of mirth, What doeth it? I sought in mine heart to give myself unto wine, yet acquainting mine heart with wisdom; and to lay hold on folly, till I might see what was that good for the sons of men, which they should do under the heaven all the days of their life. I made me great works; I builded me houses;

I planted me vineyards: I made me gardens and orchards, and I planted trees in them of all kind of fruits: I made me pools of water, to water therewith the wood that bringeth forth trees: I got me servants and maidens, and had servants born in my house; also I had great possessions of great and small cattle above all that were in Jerusalem before me: I gathered me also silver and gold, and the jewels of kings and the provinces: I got me men singers and women singers, and the delights of the sons of men—musical instruments of all sorts. So I was great, and increased more than all that were before me in Jerusalem: also my wisdom remained with me. And whatsoever mine eyes desired I kept not from them, I withheld not my heart from any joy. . . . Then I looked on all the works that my hands had wrought, and on the labor that I had labored to do: and, behold, all was vanity and vexation of spirit, and there was no profit under the sun. And I turned myself to behold wisdom, and madness, and folly. But I perceived that one event happeneth to them all. Then said I in my heart, As it happeneth to the fool, so it happeneth even to me; and why was I then more wise? Then I said in my heart, that this also is vanity. For there is no remembrance of the wise more than of the fool forever; seeing that which now is in the days to come shall all be forgotten. And how dieth the wise man? As the fool. Therefore I hated life; because the work that is wrought under the sun is grievous unto me: for all is vanity and vexation of spirit. Yea, I hated all my labor which I had taken under the sun: because I should leave it unto the man that shall be after me.

. . . For what hath man of all his labor, and of the vexation of his heart, wherein he hath labored under the sun? For all his days are sorrows, and his travail grief; yea, his heart taketh not rest in the night. This is also vanity. It is not given to a man to have the blessing that he should eat and drink, and that he should make his soul enjoy good in his labor. . . .

"All things come alike to all: there is one event to the righteous, and to the wicked; to the good and to the clean, and to the unclean; to him that sacrificeth, and to him that sacrificeth not: as is the good, so is the sinner; and he that sweareth, as he that feareth an oath. This is an evil among all things that are done under the sun, that there is one event unto all: yea, also the heart of the sons of man is full of evil, and madness is in their heart while they live, and after that they go to the dead. For to him that is joined to all the living there is hope: for a living dog is better than a dead lion. For the living know that they shall die: but the dead know not anything, neither have they any more a reward; for the memory of them is forgotten. Also their love, and their hatred, and their envy, is now perished; neither have they any more a portion forever in anything that is done under the sun."[16]

That is what Solomon or whoever wrote these words says.

And this is what Indian wisdom says:

Shakyamuni,[17] a young and happy prince from whom disease and old age and death had been hidden, goes out driving and sees a frightening old man, toothless and dribbling. The prince, from whom old age had hitherto been hidden, is astonished and asks his driver what is this and why has this man come to such a pitiful, repellent, shocking pass. And when he learns that this is the general fate of all men, and that the same unavoidably awaits a young prince, he can no longer go driving and orders them to return so he can ponder upon this. And he shuts himself up alone and thinks about it. And probably he thinks of some comfort for himself because he goes out driving again, cheerful and happy. But this time he meets a sick man. He sees an emaciated, livid, trembling man with dulled eyes. The prince from whom disease had been hidden stops and asks what is this. And when he learns that this is disease to which all men are subject, and that he himself, a healthy and happy prince, tomorrow could fall ill, again he hasn't the heart to amuse himself, orders them to return, and again seeks comfort and probably finds it, because he goes out driving a third time; but on this third time he sees another new sight; he sees them carrying something.

"What is this?"

"A dead man."

"What does dead mean?" asks the prince

They tell him that to become dead means to become what this man has become. The prince goes up to the dead man, uncovers him, and looks at him. "What will happen to him next?" the prince asks.

They tell him that they will bury him in the ground.

"Why?"

"Because he surely will never be alive again and only stink and worms will come from him."

"And is this the lot of all men? And will the same happen

to me? Will they bury me, and will I stink and be eaten by worms?"

"Yes."

"Turn back! I won't go out driving; I'll never go again."

And Shakyamuni could find no comfort in life, and he decided that life is the greatest evil and he used all the powers of his spirit to free himself from it and to free others—to free them so that after death life would not somehow be renewed, to destroy life completely, at the root. That is what all Indian wisdom says.

So those are the direct answers human wisdom gives when it answers the question of life.

"The life of the body is evil and a lie. And therefore the destruction of this life of the body is something good, and we must desire it," says Socrates.

"Life is that which ought not to be—an evil—and the going into nothingness is the sole good of life," says Schopenhauer.

"Everything in the world—folly and wisdom and riches and poverty and happiness and grief—all is vanity and nonsense. Man will die and nothing will remain. And that is foolish," says Solomon.

"One must not live with the awareness of the inevitability of suffering, weakness, old age, and death—one must free oneself from life, from all possibility of life," says Buddha.

And what these powerful intellects said was said and thought and felt by millions and millions of people like them. And I too thought and felt that.

So that my wanderings in science not only did not take me out of my despair but only increased it. One science did not answer the questions of life; another science did answer, directly confirming my despair and showing that the view I had reached wasn't the result of my delusion, of the morbid state of my mind—on the contrary, it confirmed for me what I truly thought and agreed with the conclusions of the powerful intellects of mankind.

It's no good deceiving oneself. All is vanity. Happy is he who was not born; death is better than life; one needs to be rid of life.

VII

FINDING NO EXPLANATION IN SCIENCE, I BEGAN TO LOOK for this explanation in life, hoping to find it in the people surrounding me, and I began to observe people like myself and how they lived around me and to deal with the question that had led me to despair.

And this is what I found in people of the same education and way of life as myself.

I found that for people in my world there are four ways out of the terrible position in which we all find ourselves.

The first way out is the way of ignorance. It is this: not to know, not to understand that life is evil and meaningless. People of this type—mostly women, or very young or very stupid people—haven't yet understood the question of life that showed itself to Schopenhauer, Solomon, and Buddha. They don't see either the dragon waiting for them or the mice gnawing the bushes they are clinging to, and they lick the drops of honey. But they lick these drops of honey only for a while; something will draw their attention to the dragon and the mice, and that's the end of their licking. There was nothing for me to learn from them; you should not stop knowing what you know.

The second way out is the way of Epicureanism. It is this: knowing the hopelessness of life, enjoying those good things that do exist, not looking at either dragon or mice, and licking the honey in the best possible way, especially if a lot has gathered on the bush. Solomon describes this way thus:

"Then I commended mirth, because a man hath no better thing under the sun, than to eat, and to drink, and to be merry: for that shall abide with him of his labor the days of his life, which God giveth him under the sun. . . .

"Go thy way, eat thy bread with joy, and drink thy wine with a merry heart. . . . Live joyfully with the wife whom thou lovest all the days of the life of thy vanity, which he hath given thee under the sun, all the days of thy vanity: for that is thy portion in this life, and in thy labor which thou takest under the sun. Whatsoever thy hand findeth to do, do it with thy might; for there is no work, nor device, nor knowledge, nor wisdom, in the grave, whither thou goest."[18]

Most people in our world take this way out. The conditions in which they find themselves mean that they have more good things than bad, and moral obtuseness makes it possible for them to forget that not everyone can have a thousand women and palaces like Solomon, that for every man with a thousand wives there are a thousand men without wives, and that for every palace there are a thousand men building it with the sweat of their brows, and that the chance which today has made me Solomon tomorrow can make me Solomon's slave. The obtuseness of these people's imagination makes it possible for them to forget what gave Buddha no comfort—the inevitability of illness, old age, and death that any day now will destroy all these pleasures. The fact that some of these people affirm that the obtuseness of their thought and imagination is a philosophy that they call positive does not in my view set them apart from the ranks of those who lick the honey without seeing the question. And I could not copy these people; lacking their obtuseness of imagination I could not artificially produce it in me. I could not take my eyes from the mice and the dragon, like any living man once he has seen them.

The third way out is the way of strength and energy. It is this: having understood life is evil and meaningless, to destroy it. A few strong and logical people do this. Having understood the whole stupidity of the joke played on us and having understood that the blessings of the dead are more than the blessings of the living and that it is best of all not to be, they act and put an end at once to this stupid joke, seeing that the means are there: a noose around the neck, water, a knife to pierce the heart, trains on the railways. And there are more and more people from our world acting like this. And for the most part people are taking this action at the very best period of their life, when the powers of the spirit are in their prime and few of the habits that degrade man's mind have been acquired. I saw this way out as the most worthwhile and wanted to take that action.

The fourth way out is the way of weakness. It is this: understanding the evil and meaninglessness of life, to continue to drag it out, knowing in advance that nothing will come of it. People of this type know that death is better than life, but not having the strength to act intelligently—to end the fraud quickly and kill themselves—they seem to be waiting for something. This is the way of weakness, for if I know what is best and it is in my power, why not take the best? . . . I was in this category.

So people like me are saved from a terrible dilemma by four ways out. However much I strained my mental concentration, I could not see any other way out apart from these four. The first way: not to understand that life is meaningless, vanity, and evil and that it's better not to live. I couldn't help knowing that, and once I knew it I couldn't shut my eyes to it. The second way: to make use of life as it is, not thinking of the future. That too I couldn't do. Like Shakyamuni I couldn't go hunting when I knew that there existed old age, suffering, death. My imagination was too lively. Furthermore I couldn't rejoice in the fleeting chance that for a moment threw pleasure to my lot. The third way:

having understood that life is evil and folly, to put an end to it, to kill oneself. That I understood, but for some reason I didn't kill myself yet. The fourth way: to live taking the position of Solomon and Schopenhauer; to know that life is a foolish joke played on us and still to live, wash, dress, dine, talk, and even write little books. For me that was repugnant, painful, but that was the position I took.

Now I see that if I didn't kill myself, the reason for that was a dim awareness of the wrongness of my thoughts. However convincing and unquestionable my own way of thinking and that of the wise men who had brought us to recognize the meaninglessness of life might seem to me, there remained in me a vague doubt of the truth at the starting point of my reasoning.

It was this: I, my reason, recognized that life is contrary to reason. If there is no higher reason (and there isn't and no one can prove it), then for me reason is the creator of life. If there were no reason, there would be no life for me. How can this reason deny life but be the creator of life? Or, looked at another way, if there were no life, my reason too wouldn't exist—therefore reason must be the child of life. Life is everything. Reason is the fruit of life, and now this reason is denying life itself. I felt that there was something wrong here.

"Life is a meaningless evil, that is unquestionable," I said to myself. "But I have lived, I still live, and all mankind is living and has lived. How can that be? Why does mankind live when it is able not to live? Are I and Schopenhauer alone so clever that we have understood the meaninglessness and evil of life?

"The debate about the vanity of life is not so subtle, and it has been going on a long time and by the simplest people, but they have lived and are living. So are they still living without ever having thought of doubting the rationality of life?"

My knowledge, confirmed by the wisdom of wise men, revealed to me that everything in the world—organic and inorganic—everything had been set up with exceptional intelligence, but my own situation was stupid. But these fools—the huge masses of simple people—knew nothing of how everything organic and inorganic had been set up in the world, but they lived and they thought that their own life had been set up very intelligently!

And there came into my head this: "But what if there is something else I don't know?" Now ignorance acts just like that. Ignorance always says this very thing. When it doesn't know something, it says that what it doesn't know is stupid. In actual fact the result is that here exists the whole of mankind that has ever lived and is living, apparently understanding the meaning of life, for without understanding it it could not live, but I am saying that all life is meaningless and that I cannot live.

No one prevents us from denying life with Schopenhauer. But then kill yourself—and you won't have to think. If you don't like life, kill yourself. If you're alive but you can't understand the meaning of life then put an end to it, but don't hang about in this life, telling and writing that you don't understand life. You've come into merry company; everyone feels good, everyone knows what he or she is doing, but you are bored and disgusted, so go.

So in actual fact are we, convinced of the need for suicide without taking the decision to commit it, but the weakest, most illogical, and in simple terms the most stupid of men, making a great song and dance about our own stupidity?

All of our wisdom, however unquestionably certain, has not given us knowledge of the meaning of our life. But all of mankind that constitutes life, in its millions, does not doubt the meaning of life.

In fact ever since those times long, long ago, since life has existed, of which I know anything, people have lived knowing the debate about the vanity of life that showed me its meaninglessness, but they still went on living, giving life some kind of meaning. Ever since some kind of human life began, people already had that meaning for life and they led that life, and it has come down to me. Everything that is in me and around me, all of that is the fruit of their knowledge of life. Those very tools of thought with which I discuss this life and judge it, all those have been made not by me but by them. I myself was born, educated, grew up, thanks to them. They mined iron; taught us to fell trees; tamed cattle, horses; taught us to live together, brought order to our life; they taught me to think, to speak. And I, their creation, fed by them; nursed, taught by them; thinking their thoughts and their words, have proved to them that these have no meaning! "Something is wrong here," I said to myself. "Somewhere I have made a mistake." But I could not find out where the mistake lay.

VIII

ALL THESE DOUBTS, WHICH I AM NOW CAPABLE OF expressing more or less coherently, I couldn't express then. Then I only felt that however logically inevitable my conclusions about the vanity of life, confirmed by the greatest thinkers, there was something wrong in them. Whether in the actual argument or in putting the question, I didn't know; I only felt that the force of the reasoning was complete but that that wasn't enough. All these conclusions couldn't convince me to the point that I did what followed from my reasoning—that I killed myself. And I would be telling a lie if I said that it was reason that brought me to the conclusion I reached and that I didn't kill myself. My reason was working, but something else was also working which I can only call consciousness of life. There was also a force working that made me pay attention to one thing rather than another, and that force also took me out of my desperate condition and set my reason onto a quite different course. This force made me pay attention to the fact that I and hundreds of people like me were not the whole of mankind, that I didn't yet know the life of mankind.

Looking around the close circle of my contemporaries, I only saw people who didn't understand the question; people who did understand it and drowned it in the intoxication of life; people who did understand and put an end to their lives; and people who did understand and out of weakness went on living a desperate life. And I saw no others. I thought that this narrow circle of educated, wealthy, and idle people to which I belonged constituted the whole of mankind, and that the millions of those who have lived and are living are just *those*: some kind of cattle, not people.

However strange, however incredible and incomprehensible it now seems to me that in thinking about life I could ignore the life of mankind around me on all sides; that I could so ludicrously lose my way as to think that my life, the life of the Solomons and Schopenhauers, was the real, normal life; that the life of millions was something not worth attention; however strange that is to me now, I see that it was so. In the error of my mind's pride, I thought it beyond question that I and Solomon and Schopenhauer had put the question so surely and truly that there could be no other; it seemed so beyond question that all those millions belonged to those who hadn't yet got as far as understanding the whole depth of the question, that I searched for the meaning of my own life and never thought once, "But what meaning did all the millions who have lived and are living give to their lives?"

For a long time I lived in this madness, one especially peculiar, not in words but in fact to us, the most liberal and educated people. But thanks maybe to my kind of strange physical love of the real working people that made me understand them and see that they are not as stupid as we think, or thanks to the sincerity of my conviction that I could know nothing, that the best I could do was to hang myself, I sensed that if I wanted to live and understand the meaning of life, then I must look for that meaning of life not among those who have lost the meaning of life and want to kill themselves but among those millions of people dead and alive who make life and support their own lives and ours.

And I looked around at the huge masses of people, dead and alive, simple, uneducated, not wealthy people, and I saw something quite different. I saw that all these millions of those who have lived and are living, all with few exceptions did not fit my classification, that I couldn't see them as not understanding the question because they themselves were asking it and answering it with exceptional clarity. I also couldn't see them as Epicureans because their lives were made up more of privations and sufferings than of pleasures; still less could I see them as foolishly living out a meaningless life since every act of their lives and deaths themselves were explained by them. They regarded killing oneself as the greatest evil. It proved to be the case that the whole of mankind had knowledge of the meaning of life, unrecognized and scorned by me. It turned out that rational knowledge does not give the meaning of life, it excludes life; the meaning given to life by millions of people, the whole of mankind, is founded on some kind of despised false knowledge.

Rational knowledge in the person of scholars and wise men denies the meaning of life but the great mass of people, the whole of mankind, recognizes that meaning in irrational knowledge. And that irrational knowledge is faith, the very thing I had to reject. That is God one and three, that is creation in six days, devils and angels and everything I couldn't accept as long as I didn't go mad.

My situation was terrible. I knew that I would find nothing on the path of rational knowledge but the denial of life, but there, in faith, nothing but the denial of reason, which was even more impossible than the denial of life. According to rational knowledge it turned out that life is evil and people know this, that not to live is something that depends on them, but they have lived and do live, and I myself was living although I had known long before that life is meaningless and evil. According to faith it turned out that in order to understand the meaning of life I had to renounce reason, the very thing for which meaning is needed.

IX

THERE AROSE A CONTRADICTION FROM WHICH THERE were two ways out: either what I called rational wasn't as rational as I thought; or what seemed to me irrational wasn't as irrational as I thought. And I started to test the line of reasoning of my rational knowledge.

Testing the line of reasoning of rational knowledge, I found it quite correct. The conclusion that life is nothing was unavoidable, but I saw an error. The error lay in the fact that my thinking didn't correspond to the question I had asked. The question was this: why do I live, that is, what is real and lasting that will come out of my illusory and impermanent life, what meaning does my finite existence have in this infinite world? And to answer this question I studied life.

The answering of all possible questions about life obviously could not satisfy me because my question, however simple it might appear at the beginning, included a requirement for the explanation of the finite by the infinite and the reverse.

I was asking, "What is the meaning of my life outside time, outside cause, outside space?" But I was asking the question, "What is the meaning of my life within time, within cause, and within space?" The result was that after a long labor of thought, I answered, "None."

In my reasoning I constantly equated—I couldn't do otherwise—finite with finite and infinite with infinite, and so the result I got was what it had to be: a force is a force, a substance is a substance, will is will, infinity is infinity, nothing is nothing, and there could be no further result.

Something like this happens in mathematics when, thinking you are solving an equation, you produce a solution of identity. The line of reasoning is correct but in the result you get the answer $a = a$ or $x = x$ or $0 = 0$. The same happened with my reasoning about the question of the meaning of my life. The answers given by the whole of science to the question only produced identities.

And indeed strictly rational science, which begins like Descartes[19] with completely doubting everything, rejects all the knowledge recognized by faith and constructs everything anew on the laws of reason and experience, and cannot give any other answer to the question of life but the very one I received—an indeterminate answer. It was only at the start that science seemed to me to give a positive answer—the answer of Schopenhauer: life has no meaning; it is evil. But having looked into the matter I understood that the answer isn't positive, but was just my feeling expressing it as such. A strictly expressed answer, as articulated by the Brahmins and Solomon and Schopenhauer, is only an indeterminate answer or an identity, 0 = 0; life appearing to me as nothing is nothing. So philosophical science denies nothing but only answers that it cannot solve this question, that for it the solution remains indeterminate.

Having answered this, I understood that it was impossible to look for the answer to my question in rational science, and that the answer given by rational science is only an indication that the answer can only be given with the question being put differently, only when there is introduced into the reasoning the question of the relationship of the finite to the infinite. I also understood that however irrational and distorted the answers given by faith, they have the advantage that into every answer they introduce the relationship of the finite to the infinite, without which there cannot be an answer. However I might put the question, "How should I live?" the answer is "By God's law." "What that is real will come out of my life?" "Eternal suffering or eternal bliss." "What meaning of life is there that is not destroyed by death?" "Union with the infinity of God, paradise."

So apart from rational science, which previously seemed to me the only one, I was inescapably led to recognize that the whole of living mankind has another irrational science—faith, which gives the possibility of living. All the irrationality of faith remained the same for me as before but I couldn't fail to recognize that it alone gives mankind answers to the questions of life and consequently the possibility of living.

Rational science had led me to recognize that life is meaningless; my life stopped and I wanted to destroy myself. Looking around at people, at the whole of mankind, I saw that people do live and affirm that they know the meaning of life. I looked at myself: I did live as long as I knew the meaning of life. Like others I too was given the meaning of life and the possibility of life by faith.

Looking further at people from other countries, at my contemporaries, and at those who lived before us, I saw one and the same thing. Where there is life, ever since mankind has existed faith gives the possibility of living, and the main features of faith are everywhere and always one and the same.

Whatever the faith and whatever the answers and to whomever it might give them, every answer from faith gives the finite existence of man a meaning of the infinite—a meaning that is not destroyed by suffering, privations and death. That means in faith alone can one find the meaning and potential of life. And I understood that faith in its most essential meaning is not just "the unveiling of unseen things" and so forth, it isn't revelation (that is only a description of one of the signs of faith), it's not just the relationship of man to God (one needs to define faith and then God, but not to define faith through God), it's not agreement with what one has been told by someone (as faith is most often understood)—faith is the knowledge of the meaning of man's life, as a result of which man does not destroy himself but lives. Faith is the life force. If a man lives, then he believes in something. If he didn't believe that one must live for something, then he wouldn't live. If he doesn't see and doesn't understand the illusoriness of the finite, he believes in the finite; if he does understand the illusoriness of the finite, he must believe in the infinite without which one cannot live.

And I remembered the whole course of my mental labors and I was horrified. It was now clear to me that for a man to be able to live he either had not to see the infinite or have an explanation of the meaning of life in which the finite was equated with the infinite. I had such an explanation but I had no need for it while I believed in the finite, and I began to test it by reason. And with the light of reason I found the whole of my previous explanation to dissolve in dust. But there came a time when I stopped believing in the finite. And then I began to construct out of what I knew, on rational foundations, an explanation that would give the meaning of life; but nothing got constructed. Together with mankind's best minds I came to 0 = 0 and was very surprised to get such a solution when nothing else could come of it.

What was I doing when I looked for an answer in the experimental sciences? I wanted to learn why I lived and for that I studied everything outside myself. Clearly I was able to learn a great deal, but nothing of what I needed.

What was I doing when I looked for an answer in the philosophical sciences? I studied the thoughts of those people who were in the same position as myself, who had no answer to the question, "Why do I live?" Clearly I could learn nothing other than what I myself knew: that one can know nothing.

"What am I?" "Part of the infinite." Now in those few words lies the whole problem. Can mankind have asked this question of itself only yesterday? And really did no one ask himself this question before me—such a simple question coming to the tip of the tongue of any clever child?

This question has been asked ever since man has existed; and ever since man has existed, it has been understood that for the question to be answered it has been just as inadequate to equate finite to finite and infinite to infinite, and ever since man has existed, the relationship of finite to infinite has been looked for and expressed.

All these concepts, in which the finite is equated to the infinite and the result is the meaning of life, concepts of God, freedom, good, we submit to logical analysis. And these concepts do not stand up to the criticism of reason.

If it weren't so terrible, it would be funny to see the pride and complacency with which like children we take to pieces a watch, remove the spring, make a toy of it, and then are surprised that the watch stops working.

The solution of the contradiction between finite and infinite is necessary and valuable, providing an answer to the question whereby life is made possible. And this is the only solution, one we find everywhere, always and among all peoples—a solution coming down out of time in which the life of man has been lost to us, a solution so difficult that we could make nothing like it—this solution we carelessly destroy in order to ask again that question inherent in everyone to which there is no answer.

The concepts of infinite God, of the divinity of the soul, of the link between the affairs of man and God, the concepts of moral good and evil, are concepts evolved in the distant history of man's life that is hidden from our eyes, are those concepts without which life and I myself would not be, and rejecting all this labor of all mankind, I want to do everything by myself, alone, anew, and in my own way.

I didn't think so then, but the germs of those thoughts were already in me. I understood firstly that for all our wisdom my position alongside Schopenhauer and Solomon was a stupid one: we understand that life is evil and still we live. This is clearly stupid because if life is stupid—and I do so love all that is rational—then I should clearly destroy life, and no one would be able to challenge this. Secondly I understood that all our reasoning was going around in a vicious circle, like a wheel that has come off its gear. However much, however well we reason, we cannot give an answer to the question, and it will always be 0 = 0, and so our path is likely to be the wrong one. Thirdly, I began to understand that the answers given to faith enshrine the most profound wisdom of mankind, and that I didn't have the right to deny them on the grounds of reason, and that, most importantly, these answers do answer the question of life.

X

I UNDERSTOOD THIS BUT I HAD NO RELIEF FROM IT.

I was now ready to accept my faith provided it didn't require of me a direct denial of reason, which would have been a falsehood. And I studied both Buddhism and Islam in books and above all Christianity both in books and in the living people around me.

Naturally I turned first of all to believers from my own world, to scholars, Orthodox theologians, monastic elders, Orthodox theologians of the new tendency and even so-called New Christians who preached salvation by faith in redemption. And I seized on these believers and questioned them about the nature of their belief and in what they saw the meaning of life.

In spite of making every possible concession, avoiding all disputes, I could not accept the faith of these people—I saw that what they projected as faith wasn't an explanation but an obscuring of the meaning of life, and they themselves affirmed their faith not in order to answer that question of life that had led me to faith but for some different aims alien to me.

I remember the painful feeling of horror on returning to my former despair after hope, which I felt many, many times in my dealings with these people. The more they explained their teaching, in more detail, the more clearly I saw their error and lost my hope of finding in their faith the explanation of the meaning of life.

It wasn't that in their exposition of their teaching they mixed with the Christian truths which had always been close to me many more superfluous and irrational things—it wasn't that which repelled me; I was repelled by the fact that the life of these people was the same as mine, only with the difference that it wasn't in accordance with the very principles they expounded in their teaching. I felt clearly that they were deceiving themselves, and that they like myself had no other meaning of life than to live while life is there and to take all that a hand can grasp. I saw this because if they had had that meaning of life in which the fear of privation, suffering, and death is destroyed, then they wouldn't be frightened of them. But these believers from our world, just like myself, lived in plenty; tried to increase or preserve it; were frightened of privation, suffering, death; and lived like myself and all of us unbelievers, lived satisfying their lusts, lived as badly, if not worse, than unbelievers.

No reasoning could convince me of the truth of their

faith. Only acts that would show that they had a meaning of life by which the poverty, sickness, death that terrified me did not terrify them could have convinced me. But I did not see such acts among the varied believers from our world. On the contrary I saw such acts among the most extreme unbelievers from our world but never among the so-called believers from our world.

And I understood that the faith of these people was not the faith I was seeking, that their faith was not faith but only one of the Epicurean consolations in life. I understood that this faith might serve perhaps if not for consolation then for some distraction for the repentant Solomon on his deathbed, but it cannot serve the huge majority of mankind, which is called not to amuse itself making use of the labor of others but to create life. For the whole of mankind to be able to live, for it to continue life, giving it meaning, these people, these millions must have another, a real knowledge of faith. I hadn't been convinced of the existence of faith by my own and by Solomon's and Schopenhauer's failure to kill ourselves but by the fact that these millions have lived and are living and bear us along with the Solomons on the waves of their lives.

And I began to come close to believers from among poor, simple people, wandering pilgrims, monks, dissenters, peasants. The teaching of these ordinary people was also Christian like the teaching of the false believers from our world. A great many superstitions too were mixed in with Christian truths, but the difference lay in that for them the superstitions of believers from our world were quite superfluous, didn't connect with their lives, were only a kind of Epicurean amusement; whereas the superstitions of believers from the working people were connected to their lives to such an extent that it was impossible to imagine their lives without these superstitions—they were an essential condition of this life. The whole life of believers from our world was a contradiction of their faith, but the whole life of the laboring believers was a confirmation of the meaning of life given by the knowledge of faith. And I began to look into the life and beliefs of these people and the more I looked the more I was convinced that they had true faith, that their faith was essential to them and alone gave them the meaning and the possibility of life. By contrast with what I saw in our world, where it is possible to live without faith and where barely one in a thousand professes himself a believer, among these people there is barely a single unbeliever among thousands. By contrast with what I saw in our world, where all of life passes in idleness, amusements, and discontent with life, I saw that the whole life of these people passed in heavy labor, and they were less discontented with life than the wealthy. By contrast with people of our world, who resisted and were indignant at fate for privation and suffering, these people accepted illness and sorrows without any bewilderment or resistance but with a calm and firm conviction that all this must be and cannot be otherwise, that this is good. By contrast with us, who the cleverer we are the less we understand the meaning of life and see some wicked joke in the fact that we suffer and die, these people live, suffer, and approach death with calm, most often with joy. By contrast with our world, where a calm death, a death without terror and despair, is a very rare exception, a death without calm, without humility, without joy is a very rare exception among ordinary people. And such people, deprived of everything which for Solomon and ourselves is the sole good of life, are the great multitude. I looked more widely around me. I looked into the lives of the great masses of people past and present. And I saw that those who understood the meaning of life, who knew how to live and die were not two or three or ten but hundreds, thousands, millions. And all of them, endlessly various in character, intellect, education, position, all identically and in contrast to my own ignorance, knew the meaning of life and death, calmly labored, endured privation and suffering, lived and died, seeing in that not "vanity" but good.

And I came to love these people. The more I entered into their lives and the lives of dead people like them of whom I had read and heard, the more I loved them and the easier it became for me myself to live. I lived like that for two years and a transformation happened to me that had been coming for a long time and the seeds of which had always been in me. What happened to me is that the life of our world—of wealthy, educated people—not only became loathsome to me but lost all meaning. All our actions, reasoning, science, art—all that seemed to me just indulgence. I understood that one could not look for meaning in that. The activities of the working people, creating life, seemed to me the only true work. And I understood that the meaning given to that life is the truth and I accepted it.

XI

AND REMEMBERING THAT THESE VERY BELIEFS HAD repelled me and seemed to me meaningless when they were professed by people whose lives contradicted these beliefs, and how these very beliefs attracted me and seemed to me to make sense when I saw that people lived by them, I understood why I then had rejected these beliefs and why I had found them meaningless but now accepted them and found them full of meaning. I understood that I had erred and how I had erred. I erred not so much because I thought wrongly as because I lived badly. I understood that the truth was hidden from me not so much by the error of my thinking as by my life itself in the exclusive conditions of Epicureanism and of satisfying my lusts in which I spent it. I understood that my question of what is my life and the answer, evil, were quite right. What was wrong was just that the answer that only applied to me I applied to life in general: I asked myself what is my life and got the answer, evil and meaningless. And indeed my life—a life of pandering to lust—was meaningless and evil, and therefore the answer "life is evil and meaningless" applied only to my life and not to human life as a whole.

I understood that truth I later found in the Gospels, that people loved darkness rather than the light because their actions were evil. For everyone whose actions are evil hates the light and does not go toward it so that his actions are not revealed. I understood that to understand the meaning of life, first life must not be meaningless and evil, then one can use reason to understand it. I understood why I had spent so long going about near such an obvious truth, and that if one is to think and speak about the life of mankind, then one must speak and think about the life of mankind but not about the life of a few parasites on life. This truth is always a truth, just as $2 \times 2 = 4$, but I did not recognize it, because in recognizing that $2 \times 2 = 4$, I would have had to recognize that I am not good. And to feel myself good was more important and compelling than $2 \times 2 = 4$. I came to love good people, hated myself, and I recognized the truth. Now everything became clear to me.

What if an executioner who spent his life in torture and decapitation, or a hopeless drunk, or a madman shut up in a dark room for his entire life, looking around his room and imagining that he would perish if he left it—what if they asked themselves, "What is life?". Obviously to the question "What is life?" they could not get any other answer but one stating that life is the greatest evil; and the madman's answer would be completely correct, but only for him. What if I am a madman like him? What if we all, wealthy, educated people, are madmen like him?

And I understood that we are indeed madmen like him.

I surely was a madman like him. And in fact a bird exists so that it must fly, gather food, build nests, and when I see a bird doing this, I rejoice in its joy. A goat, a hare, a wolf exist so that they must feed, multiply, feed their families, and when they do this I am firmly aware that they are happy and their lives make sense. What must a man do? He must make his living just like the animals, but only with the difference that he will perish making it on his own—he must make it not for himself but for all. And when he does this, I am firmly aware that he is happy and his life makes sense. What had I done during my thirty years of conscious life? I not only did not make a living for all, I didn't even make it for myself. I lived as a parasite and having asked myself, "Why do I live?" I got the answer, "To no purpose." If the meaning of man's life lies in making that living, then how could I, who had spent thirty years not making a living but destroying it for myself and others, get any other answer but that my life is meaningless and evil? And it was meaningless and evil.

The life of the world happens in accordance with someone's will—someone achieves his purpose with this life of the whole world and with our lives. To have a hope of understanding the meaning of that will, one must first fulfill it—do what is wanted of us. But if I won't do what is wanted of me, then I will never understand either what is wanted of me or even less what is wanted of us all and of the whole world.

If a naked, hungry beggar is brought from a crossroads to a covered place in a fine establishment, given food and drink, and made to move a stick up and down, then obviously, before finding out why he has been taken, why he is moving the stick, whether the organization of the whole establishment makes sense, the beggar must first of all move the stick. If he moves the stick, then he will see that the stick moves a pump, that the pump pumps up water, that the water goes over the garden beds; then he'll be taken from the covered well and put onto different work, and he will gather the fruits and enter into his master's joy, and as he moves from lower work to higher, having an ever deeper understanding of the organization of the whole establishment and taking part in it, he will never think of asking why he is here, nor will he start blaming the master.

In the same way the simple, uneducated working people who do the master's will, whom we think of as cattle, do not blame him; but here we are, the wise men, eating away our master's food but doing nothing of what the master wants from us, and instead of doing it, we sit down in a circle and argue, "Why move the stick? It's stupid." What a conclusion. And we've concluded that the master is stupid or that he doesn't exist, while we are intelligent, only we feel that we are quite useless and we must somehow be rid of ourselves.

XII

MY AWARENESS OF THE ERROR OF RATIONAL KNOWLedge freed me from the temptation of idle theorizing. My conviction that one can only find knowledge of the truth in life made me doubt the rightness of my own life; but I was only saved by pulling myself in time out of my exclusiveness and seeing the true life of simple working people and understanding that only this was the true life. I understood that if I want to understand life and its meaning, I must live not the life of a parasite but the true life, and having accepted the meaning given it by true mankind and having merged myself with this life, to test it.

At that time the following happened to me. During all that year when I was asking myself every minute whether I should end it by a noose or a bullet—during all that time, alongside those ways of thought and observation of which I was speaking, my heart was suffering from a feeling of torment. This feeling I can only call the search for God.

I say that this search was not a process of rational thought but a feeling because this search did not come out of my way of thinking—it was even directly opposed to it—but it came out of my heart. It was a feeling of terror, of being orphaned, of being alone among everything alien, and of hope for someone's help.

Although I was completely convinced of the impossibility of proving the existence of a god (Kant[20] had proved to me that one cannot prove this, and I fully understood him) I still sought God; I hoped I would find him and by old habit I turned with prayer to what I sought and did not find. Sometimes I would test in my mind the arguments of Kant and Schopenhauer about the impossibility of proving the existence of a god, and sometimes I started to refute them. Cause, I said to myself, isn't the same category of thought as space and time. If I exist, then for that there is a cause, and for causes there is a cause. And this cause of everything is what they call God; and I stopped at that thought and tried with all my being to become aware of the presence of this cause. And as soon as I became aware that there was a power holding me, I at once felt the possibility of life. But I asked myself, "What is this cause, this power? How should I think of it, how should I relate to what I call God?" And only the familiar answers came into my mind: "He is the creator, the all-provident." These answers didn't satisfy me, and I felt that what I needed for life was disappearing within me. I became terrified and began to pray to him whom I sought for him to help me. And the more I prayed, the clearer it was to me that he wasn't hearing me and that there was no one to whom I could turn. And with this despair in my heart that there is no God, none, I said, "Lord, have mercy, save me! Lord, teach me, my god!" But no one had mercy on me and I felt that my life was ending.

But again and again from different sides I came to recognize that I could not have appeared in the world without any reason, cause, and meaning, that I could not be such a fledgling fallen from the nest as I felt myself to be. Yes, a fledgling fallen from the nest, I lie on my back and cheep in the long grass, but I cheep because I know that my mother carried me in her, hatched me, warmed me, fed me, loved me. Where is she, that mother of mine? I have been abandoned; who abandoned me? I cannot hide from myself the fact that someone gave birth to me in love. Who is this someone? Again, God.

"He knows and sees my searching, despair, struggle. He is," I said to myself. And I only had to recognize this for a moment for life at once to rise up within me, and I felt both the possibility and the joy of existence. But again from recognizing the existence of God I moved on to searching for how I should relate to him, and again I imagined that God, our creator in three persons, who sent his son, the redeemer. And again this god, a god separate from the world, from me, melted like a block of ice, melted before my eyes, and again nothing remained, and again the source of life dried up; I went into despair and felt that there was nothing for me to do but kill myself. And, worst of all, I felt that I couldn't even do that.

Not twice, not three times, but tens and hundreds of times I came into these moods—now of joy and animation, then again of despair and an awareness of the impossibility of life.

I remember it was early spring; I was alone in the forest, listening to the sounds of the forest. I listened and kept thinking of one thing, just as I had thought constantly of one and the same thing during these last three years. I again sought God.

"Very well, there is no God," I said to myself. "There is none who would not be my imagined creation but reality, like my whole life; there is none. And nothing, no miracles can prove such a god, because miracles will be my imagined creation, and irrational as well."

"But what about my idea of God, the one whom I seek?" I asked myself. "Where did this idea come from?" And again at this thought joyous waves of life surged up within me. Everything around me took on life, acquired meaning. But my joy did not last long. My mind continued its work. "The idea of God is not God," I said to myself. "The idea is what takes place within me, the idea of God is what I can rouse or not rouse within me. It is not what I am seeking. I am seeking that without which there can be no life." And again everything started to die around me and within me, and again I wanted to kill myself.

But here I looked at myself, at what was happening within me, and I remembered all those hundreds of times I had died and come to life again. I remembered that I lived only when I believed in God. As it was before, so it is now, I said to myself: I only have to know of God and I live; I only have to forget him and I die. What is this dying and coming to life again? Clearly I do not live when I lose my faith in the existence of God, clearly I would have killed myself long ago if I didn't have a dim hope of finding him. Clearly I do live, truly live, only when I feel him and seek him. "So what more do I seek?" a voice cried in me. So there he is. He is that without which one cannot live. To know God and to live are one and the same. God is life.

"Live seeking God, and then there will be no life without God." And more strongly than ever everything was lit up within me and around me, and this light now did not leave me.

And I was saved from suicide. When and how this change took place in me I could not say. Just as slowly and imperceptibly as the life force had been destroyed in me and I had come to the impossibility of living, to the stopping of life, to the need for suicide, so gradually and imperceptibly this life force came back to me. And it's strange that the life force that came back to me wasn't a new one but the oldest—the very one that had sustained me in the earliest times of my life. In everything I returned to what I had known before, in childhood and in youth. I returned to belief in the will that had produced me and wanted something of me; I turned to making the chief goal of my life to do better, to live more in accordance with this will; I returned to being able to find the expression of this will in what all of mankind had evolved for its guidance in the places that had been hidden from me; I returned to belief in God, in moral perfection, and in tradition that handed down the meaning of life. Only there was the difference that then all that had been accepted unconsciously whereas now I knew that without this I could not live.

There happened to me something like this: I was put into a boat—I don't remember when—pushed off from some shore I didn't know, given a direction to the other bank, given oars into my untrained hands, and left alone. I toiled as best I could and rowed with the oars, but the further I rowed out into the middle, the faster became the current taking me away from my goal and the more often I came across rowers like myself carried away by the current. There were single oarsmen carrying on rowing; there were other rowers who had thrown away their oars; there were big boats, great ships full of people; some fought the current, others surrendered to it. And the more I rowed, the more I looked downstream at the streaming mass of all the rowers, I forgot the directions I had been given. In the very middle of the stream, in the throng of boats and ships being carried downstream, I completely lost my way and threw away my oars. On every side around me amid cheer and exultation they went on downstream by oar and sail, assuring me and each other that there could be no other way. And I believed them and went with them on the flow. And I was carried far, so far that I heard the noise of the rapids in which I would be wrecked, and I saw boats that had been wrecked in them. And I recovered my senses. For a long time I could not understand what had happened to me. Ahead of me I saw only the doom toward which I was speeding and of which I was frightened. I saw no salvation anywhere and I didn't know what to do. But looking back I saw countless boats fighting against the current without stopping, I remembered the shore, the oars, and the directions, and I started to row back upstream and toward the shore.

The shore was God, the directions were tradition, the oars were the freedom given me to row away toward the shore, to be united with God. And so the life force was renewed in me and I began to live again.

XIII

I RENOUNCED THE LIFE OF OUR WORLD, HAVING COME to recognize that this is not life but only a simulation of life; that the conditions of excess in which we live deprive us of the possibility of understanding life; and that in order to understand life I must understand not a life of exceptions, not the life of us, parasites on life, but the life of the simple working people, those who live life and the meaning they give it. The simple working people around me were the Russian people, and I turned to them and to the meaning they gave life. This meaning, if one can put it into words, was the following: Every man has come into the world by God's will. And God has so created man that every man can destroy his soul or save it. Man's task in life is to save the soul; to save his soul he must live God's way, and to live God's way he must renounce all the pleasures of life, labor, submit, endure, and be merciful. This meaning the people draw from all the Christian teaching handed down to them in the past and now, by pastors and by the tradition living in the people and expressed in legends, proverbs, and stories. But indissolubly bound up with this meaning of the popular faith, the nondissenting folk among whom I lived had much that repelled me and seemed impossible to explain: sacraments, church services, fasts, the bowing down to relics and icons. The people cannot separate one from the other, nor could I. However strange I found much of what went into the people's faith, I accepted everything, went to the services, said prayers morning and evening, fasted, prepared for communion, and at first my reason didn't resist anything. What had previously seemed to me impossible now aroused no opposition in me.

My attitude to faith now and my attitude then were quite different. Previously life itself had seemed to me full of meaning and faith, as the arbitrary affirmation of some irrational propositions, seemed absolutely superfluous as far as I was concerned and with no connection to life. I asked myself then what meaning these propositions had and, convinced that they didn't have any, rejected them. Now, on the contrary, I firmly knew that my life had no meaning and cannot have any, and the propositions of faith not only did not appear superfluous but I was led by unquestionable experience to the conviction that only these propositions of faith give meaning to life. Previously I regarded them as completely superfluous hieroglyphics; now if I didn't understand them I still knew that in them was meaning and said to myself that I must learn to understand them.

I reasoned as follows. I said to myself: The knowledge of faith rises, like all of mankind with its reason, from a mysterious beginning. The beginning is God, the beginning of man's body and mind. Just as my body has descended to me from God, so have my reason and my comprehension of life descended to me, and therefore all the stages of development of this comprehension cannot be false. Everything that people truly believe must be the truth; the truth can be expressed in various ways but it cannot be a lie, and therefore if it appears to me as a lie, that only means that I don't understand it. Furthermore, I said to myself, the essence of my faith lies in its giving life a meaning that is not destroyed with death. Of course, for faith to be able to answer the questions of a tsar dying in luxury, of an old slave worn out by toil, of a simple child, a wise elder, a crazy old woman, a happy young woman, a youth torn by passions, of all people with the most diverse conditions of life and education—of course, if there is a single answer answering the eternal sole question of life, "What do I live for, what will come of my life?"—that answer, though single in its essence, must be endlessly diverse in its manifestations; and the more single, the more true, the deeper this answer, of course the stranger and the more distorted it must appear as it tries to express itself according to the education and social conditions of each man. But these arguments, which justified for me the ritual side of faith, were still not enough to let me perform acts about which I had doubts in the most important matter of my life, in faith. I wished to merge with the people with all the power of my spirit, performing the ritual side of their faith, but I could not do that. I felt that I would be lying in my own eyes, would be mocking what I held sacred, if I did that. But here our new Russian theological writing came to my aid.

According to the explanation of these theologians the fundamental dogma of faith is the infallible church. From the acceptance of this dogma there comes as a necessary consequence the truth of all that the church professes. The church, as an assembly of believers united by love and therefore having true knowledge, became the foundation of my faith. I said to myself that God's truth cannot be available just to one man; it discloses itself only to the whole totality of people united by love. To comprehend the truth one must not stand apart, and in order not to stand apart one must love and accept what one may not agree with. Truth discloses itself to love and so if you don't submit to the rituals of the church, you destroy love; and in destroying love you deprive yourself of the possibility of knowing the truth. I didn't see then the sophistry expressed in this argument. I didn't see then that being united in love can give very great love but surely not the divine truth expressed in the precise words of the Nicene Creed; I did not see that love cannot make a particular expression of the truth an essential condition of unity. I did not see then the error of this argument, and thanks to it I found it possible to accept and perform all the rituals of the Orthodox Church without understanding most of them. I tried then with all the powers of my spirit to avoid any arguments and contradictions, and tried to explain rationally insofar as it was possible the church's propositions with which I came into conflict.

In performing the rituals of the church I restrained my reason and submitted to the tradition held by all mankind. I was united with my ancestors, with my loved ones—father, mother, grandfathers, grandmothers. They and those who had gone before believed and lived, and produced me. I was united too with all the millions from the ordinary people whom I respected. Besides, these actions in themselves had nothing wrong about them (I considered indulgence in lusts as wrong). Getting up early for a church service, I knew that I was doing good just because in order to humble my pride of mind, to draw closer to my ancestors and contemporaries, I was sacrificing bodily comfort for the sake of finding the meaning of life. That was the case with preparing for communion, with saying the daily prayers and performing the ritual prostrations, with observing all the fasts. However slight these sacrifices, they were sacrifices in the name of good. I prepared for communion, fasted, said the prayers at the appointed times at home and in church. Listening to the church services I uttered every word and gave them meaning when I could. In the Mass the most important words for me were: "Let us love one another of one mind . . . " The following words, "We believe in the Father, the Son and the Holy Spirit," I omitted because I could not understand them.

XIV

I HAD SUCH A NEED THEN TO BELIEVE IN ORDER TO live, but I unconsciously concealed from myself the contradictions and obscurities of Christian teaching. But this giving of meaning to the rituals had limits. If the main words of the Litany became clearer and clearer to me, if I somehow explained to myself the words, "Remembering our most Holy Lady the Mother of God and all the saints, let us give ourselves and one another and our whole life to Christ the Lord," if I explained the frequent repetitions of prayers for the tsar and his family by their being more open to temptation than others and therefore more in need of prayers, if I explained the prayers about trampling our foe and adversary beneath our feet, if I explained them by the fact of evil being that enemy—those other prayers, like the cherubim and the whole sacrament of oblation and "the chosen warriors" and the like, which make up two-thirds of all services, either had no explanation or else I felt as I brought explanation to them that I was lying and by that completely destroying my relationship to God, completely losing any possibility of faith.

I felt the same in celebrating the major church feasts. To remember the Sabbath, that is, to devote a day to turning to God, I found understandable. But the chief feast day was a remembrance of the resurrection, the reality of which I could not imagine and understand. And this name of resurrection was also given to the day celebrated every week.[21] And on those days there took place the sacrament of the Eucharist, which was completely incomprehensible to me. The other twelve feast days apart from Christmas commemorated miracles, something I was trying not to think about so as not to deny them—the Ascension, Pentecost, the Epiphany, the feast of the Intercession of the Holy Virgin, etc. In celebrating these feasts, feeling that importance was being given to what was for me the opposite of important, I either invented palliative explanations or I shut my eyes so as not to see what was tempting me.

This happened to me most strongly when taking part in the most usual sacraments, those considered to be the most important, baptism and taking communion. Here I came up against actions that weren't incomprehensible but wholly comprehensible; these actions I found tempting and I was put into a dilemma—either to lie or to reject them.

I will never forget the feeling of torment I underwent when I took communion for the first time in many years. The services, confession, the ritual prayers—all that I could understand and brought about within me the joyous recognition of the meaning of life opening up to me. Taking communion itself I explained to myself as an action commemorating Christ and signifying cleansing from sin and a full understanding of Christ's teaching. If this explanation was artificial I didn't notice its artificiality. I was so full of joy, submitting and humbling myself before the confessor, a simple, timid priest, and exposing all the filth of my soul; I was so full of joy at my thoughts merging with the aspirations of the fathers who wrote the ritual prayers; I was so full of joy to be one with all believers, past and present, that I did not feel the artificiality of my explanation. But when I went up to the "Tsar's Gates"[22] the priest made me repeat what I believe, that what I swallow is true flesh and blood, and I felt cut to the heart; it wasn't just a false note struck, it was a brutal requirement of someone who clearly had never known what faith is.

But now I let myself say it was a brutal requirement; then I didn't even think that, it was just inexpressibly painful for me. I was no longer in the situation I had been in my younger days, thinking that everything in life was clear; I had come to faith because apart from faith I had found nothing, really nothing but annihilation, so I couldn't reject this faith and I submitted. And I found a feeling in my soul that helped me to bear it. This was a feeling of self-abasement and humility. I humbled myself; I swallowed this flesh and blood without any feeling of blasphemy, with the desire to believe, but the blow had been struck. And knowing in advance what was waiting for me, I could no longer go a second time.

I continued in the same way to perform the rituals of the church precisely and still believed that in the Christian teaching I followed lay the truth, and something happened to me that now I find clear but then seemed strange.

I was listening to an illiterate peasant pilgrim talking about God, about faith, about life, about salvation, and knowledge of the truth was revealed to me. I became close to the people as I listened to his views on life and faith, and more and more I came to understand the truth. The same happened to me during a reading of Chetyi-Minei and the Prologues;[23] this became my favorite reading. Apart from miracles, which I regarded as fables to express thoughts, this reading revealed to me the meaning of life. There were the lives of Macarius the Great, of Prince Joseph (the story of Buddha), there were the words of John Chrysostom; there were the stories of the traveler in the well, of the monk who found gold, of Peter the publican; there was the story of the martyrs who all declared the same thing, that death does not exclude life; there were stories of the salvation of men who were illiterate and foolish and knew nothing of the teachings of the church.

But I only had to meet educated believers or take up their books to find some doubts in myself rise up in me with dissatisfaction and and an angry desire for argument, and I felt that the deeper I entered into their words, the further I went from the truth and walked toward the abyss.

XV

HOW OFTEN I ENVIED THE PEASANTS FOR THEIR ILLITeracy and lack of education. The statements of faith, which for me produced nonsense, for them produced nothing false; they could accept them and could believe in the truth, that truth in which I too believed. Only for me in my misery it was clear that the truth was interwoven by the thinnest of threads with lies and that I could not accept it in that form.

I lived like that for three years,[24] and at the beginning—when as a catechumen[25] I only gradually came to know the truth, just going guided by instinct to where I thought there was more light—these conflicts struck me less. When I didn't understand something I said to myself, "I'm at fault,

I am wrong." But the more I began to be imbued with these truths I was studying and the more they became the foundation of my life, the more burdensome and painful these conflicts became and the sharper became the dividing line between what I didn't understand and what couldn't be understood except by lying to myself.

In spite of these doubts and suffering I still adhered to Orthodoxy. But questions of life arose that had to be answered, and here the answer to these questions by the church—one that was the opposite of the foundations of faith by which I lived—finally made me renounce the possibility of communion with Orthodoxy. These questions were firstly the attitude of the Orthodox church to other churches—to Catholicism and the so-called schismatics. At that time as a consequence of my interest in faith I became close to believers of various denominations: to Catholics, Protestants, Old Believers, Molokans,[26] etc. And among them I met many people of high morality who were truly believers. I wanted to be a brother to these people. And what happened? The teaching that had promised me to unite all in a single faith and love, this very teaching in the person of its best representatives told me that these were all people dwelling in falsehood, that what gave them life was a temptation of the devil and that we alone were in possession of the one possible truth. And I saw that the Orthodox consider all those who do not profess a faith identical to theirs to be heretics, exactly as the Catholics and the others consider Orthodoxy to be heresy; I saw that Orthodoxy, although it tries to conceal it, has a hostile attitude to all who do not profess their faith by external symbols and words like Orthodoxy, and that is, as it has to be, firstly because the affirmation that you dwell in falsehood whereas I dwell in truth requires the harshest words that man can say to another, and secondly because a man who loves his children and brothers must have a hostile attitude to those who would turn his children and brothers to a false faith. And this hostility increases with a greater knowledge of Christian teaching. And I, who supposed truth lay in the unity of love, was involuntarily struck by the fact that this very Christian teaching was destroying what it should be producing.

This temptation is so obvious, so obvious to us, educated people living in countries where different faiths are professed, who see the scornful, arrogant, unshakeable rejection with which Catholics meet Orthodox and Protestants, with which Orthodox meet Catholics and Protestants and Protestants meet both, and the very similar attitude of Old Believers, Pashkovites[27] and Shakers, that the very obviousness of the temptation is at first puzzling. You say to yourself, "It can't be that it is so simple and that still people do not see that if two affirmations contradict each other, then neither one nor the other can hold the unified truth that faith must be. There is something here. There is some explanation." And I thought that there was and looked for this explanation and read all I could on this subject and consulted all those I could. And I got no explanation other than the very one by which the Sumsky Hussars think the Sumsky Hussars the best regiment in the world but the Yellow Uhlans think the best regiment in the world is the Yellow Uhlans. The clergy of all the various denominations, their best representatives, only told me that they believed that they dwelt in truth and the others in error, and that all they could do was pray for them. I went to see archimandrites, archpriests, elders, and hermits,[28] and no one made any attempt to explain this temptation to me. Just one of them did explain it all to me but explained it in such a way that I didn't ask anyone else.

I said that for every unbeliever who turns to the faith (and all our young generation is liable to do this) the question that puts itself first is: Why is truth held not by Lutheranism, not by Catholicism, but by Orthodoxy? He has been taught in the gymnasium and he cannot help but know what the peasant doesn't know, that Protestants and Catholics just as firmly affirm the sole truth of their faith. Historical evidence, twisted by every denomination to its own interest, is not enough. Might one not, I said, understand the teaching at a higher plane so that at that plane all differences in the teaching disappear, as they disappear for the true believer? Can we not go further along the path we are taking with the Old Believers? They affirmed that they have a different cross and hallelujahs and way of processing around the altar. We said: "You believe in the Nicene Creed and the seven sacraments, and we believe in them. Let us abide by that but for the rest do what you want." We have united with them by putting the essentials in faith above the inessentials. Now with the Catholics, can't we say: "You believe in this and that, the most important things, but as for the *filioque*[29] and the pope do what you want?" Cannot we say the same to the Protestants, being united with them on the main points? The priest I was talking to agreed with my way of thinking but said to me that such concessions would bring about censure on the religious authorities for renouncing the faith of our ancestors and would bring about a schism, and the mission of the religious authorities is to guard in all its purity the Greco-Russian Orthodox faith that has been handed down by our ancestors.

And I understood it all. I am seeking faith, the life force, but they are seeking the best way of fulfilling certain human obligations to other men. And in fulfilling these human matters they fulfill them in a human way. However much they talked of their feeling for their lost brethren, of their prayers for them raised to the throne of the Almighty, for the fulfillment of human matters one needs force, and it has always been applied, is being applied, and will be applied. If two denominations think themselves to dwell in truth and the other in error, then wanting to bring brethren to the truth, they will preach their teachings. But if false teachings are preached by the simple sons of the church, which dwells in truth, then this church must burn books and expel the man who leads her sons into temptation. What should one do with a man, a sectarian burning with the fire of a faith that is false in the eyes of Orthodoxy, who in the most important matter of life, in faith, is leading the sons of the church into temptation? What should one do with him but cut off his head or imprison him? In the reign of Alexis Mikhailovich[30] they burned men at the stake, that is, they used the severest punishment of the law at the time; in our time they also use our severest punishment—solitary confinement. And I paid attention to what was being done in the name of religion and I was appalled, and already then I almost renounced Orthodoxy. The second attitude of the Church to the questions of life was its attitude to war and capital punishment.

At that time Russia was fighting a war.[31] And Russians began to kill their brethren in the name of Christian love. It was impossible not to think about that. It was also impossible not to see that killing is an evil, is against the very first foundations of every faith. And furthermore they offered prayers in the churches for the success of our arms, and the teachers of the faith acknowledged this killing as something coming out of faith. And it wasn't just these killings in war but during the disturbances following the war that I saw members of the church, its teachers, monks, hermits, welcoming the killing of lost and helpless young men.[32] And I paid attention to everything that was being done by people professing Christianity and I was appalled.

XVI

AND I STOPPED HAVING DOUBTS AND I WAS COMPLETELY certain that in the teaching of the church to which I belonged not everything was truth. Once I would have said that all religious teaching is false; but now it was impossible to say that. Without any doubt, all ordinary people had knowledge of the truth, otherwise they couldn't have lived. Furthermore this knowledge of the truth was already open to me; I was already living by it and felt its full force, but this knowledge held falsehood too. And about that I could have no doubts. And everything that had previously repelled me now stood vividly before me. Although I saw that in all ordinary people there was less of the mixture of falsehood that had repelled me than in the representatives of the church, I nonetheless saw that in the people's faith falsehood was mixed with truth.

But where did the falsehood come from, and where did the truth come from? Both falsehood and truth had been handed down by what is called the church. Both falsehood and truth are contained in tradition, in the so-called sacred tradition and holy writ.

And willy-nilly I was drawn to the study and analysis of these writings and tradition—the analysis of which had hitherto so scared me.

And I turned to the study of that very theology I had once so scornfully rejected as superfluous. Then it had seemed to me a series of superfluous nonsense, then I had been surrounded on all sides by manifestations of life that I found clear and full of meaning; now I would have been glad to reject anything that didn't fit into a healthy mind, but I couldn't find a way for myself. The unified knowledge of the meaning of life that had been revealed to me was based on this Christian teaching, or at any rate indissolubly tied to it. However strange it might seem to my dull old mind this was the only hope of salvation. I had to examine it carefully, attentively, in order to understand it, and not even to understand it as I understood a proposition of science. I was not looking for that, and could not be looking for that, knowing the special nature of knowledge of faith. I was not going to look for the explanation of everything. I knew that the explanation of everything, like the origin of everything, must be hidden in infinity. But I wanted to understand in such a way as to be led to what has to be inevitably inexplicable, I wanted everything inexplicable to be so not because the demands of my intellect were wrong (they are right and I cannot understand anything without them) but because I saw the limitations of my intellect. I wanted to understand so that every inexplicable proposition appeared to me as the necessary consequences of reason but not as a duty of faith.

I have no doubt that religious teaching holds truth but also no doubt that it holds falsehood, and I must find truth and falsehood and separate one from the other. And so I have set myself to that task. The falsehood I have found in the teaching, the truth I have found, and the conclusions I have reached from the following parts of this work, which if it is worth it and someone needs it will probably be published some time, somewhere.

THAT WAS WRITTEN by me three years ago.

Now the other day, as I was reading over these printed

pages and returning to this way of thinking and the feelings I had within me as I was living through this, I had a dream. This dream expressed for me in compressed form everything I had experienced and described, and so I think for those too who have understood me a description of this dream will illuminate, clarify, and bring together everything that has been told at length in these pages. Here is the dream: I see that I am lying on a bed. I feel neither comfortable nor uncomfortable; I am lying on my back. But I start wondering if I am comfortable lying there; and I think that something is uncomfortable underneath my legs—whether it's too short or uneven, something is uncomfortable; I move my legs about and at the same time I start thinking about how and on what I am lying, which hadn't come into my head before. And looking at my bed I see I am lying on cords of plaited rope fastened to the sides of the bed. My feet are lying on one such cord, the calves of my legs on another; my legs are uncomfortable. For some reason I know that one can shift these cords. And with a movement of my legs I push away the last cord under them. I think it will be more comfortable like that. But I have pushed it too far; I try to catch it with my legs, but with that movement another cord slips out from underneath my shins and my legs are hanging down. I make a movement with my whole body to right myself, quite confident that I'll manage that right away, but with this movement other cords slip out and change their position underneath me, and I see that things are going quite wrong; the whole lower part of my body is moving down and hanging and my legs aren't reaching the ground. I am holding on here just by the upper part of my back, and I am beginning to feel not just uncomfortable but frightened of something. It's only at this point that I ask myself something that previously hadn't come into my head. I ask myself, where am I and on what am I lying? I begin to look around and first of all I look down, in the direction in which my body is hanging and where I feel I must fall any moment. I look down and I can't believe my eyes. It's not just that I am at a height like that of the highest pinnacle, but I am at such a height as I could never have imagined.

I can't even make out anything there down below, in that bottomless chasm above which I am hanging and into which I am being pulled. My heart contracts and I feel terror. It's terrifying to look there. If I look there I feel that I'll at once slip off the last cords and perish. I don't look, but not to look is even worse because I am thinking of what will happen to me now when I come off the last cords. And I feel that I am losing my last strength from terror and slowly slipping lower and lower on my back. Another minute and I'll come off. And then a thought comes to me: This cannot be true. This is a dream. Wake up. I try to wake up and I can't. What am I to do, what am I to do, I ask myself and wake up. Above me too there is infinite space. I look into this infinite space of the heavens and try to forget about the abyss below, and indeed I do forget. The infinite space below repels and terrifies me; the infinite space above attracts and strengthens me. I am still hanging above the chasm on the last cords that haven't yet slipped out from under me; I know that I am hanging but

I only look up and my terror passes. As happens in a dream, a voice is saying, "Watch this, this is it!" and I keep looking more and more deeply into the infinite space above and I feel that I am calmed; I remember everything that has happened and I remember how it all happened: how I moved my legs, how I hung there, how I was terrified, and how I was saved from the terror by starting to look up. And I ask myself, "Well, and what next? I am still hanging." And I don't so much look around as feel with my whole body the point of support on which I am being held. And I see that I'm no longer hanging or falling but am being held firmly. I ask myself how I'm being held; I feel, I look, and I see that under me, under the middle of my body, there is a single cord, and that looking up I am lying on it in the most stable equilibrium, and that it alone was holding me before. And here, as happens in dreams, the mechanism by which I am being held appears to me very natural, understandable, and unquestionable although if I'm awake this mechanism makes no sense. In the dream I am even surprised that I didn't understand it before. It turns out that at the head of my bed there stands a pillar, and the strength of this pillar goes without question although there is nothing for this thin pillar to stand on. Then from this pillar a loop of rope has somehow been let down very cleverly and at the same time very simply, and if you lie on this loop with the middle of your body and look up, then there can't even be a question of falling. All this was clear to me, and I was glad and calm. And someone seems to be saying to me, "Watch, remember." And I wake up.

NOTES

1 university: Tolstoy only completed the first two years of the law course of Kazan University and left without taking a degree in 1847.

2 brothers: Nikolay (1823–60), Sergey (1826–1904), and Dmitry (1827–56).

3 Musin-Pushkin: M. N. Musin-Pushkin, a member of a prominent noble family, had been appointed warden of the University of Kazan in 1827.

4 Voltaire: Prince Nikolayevich Sergeyevich Volkonsky from whom Tolstoy inherited the Yasnaya Polyana estate was a Voltairean, like many of his class, and bequeathed a fine Enlightenment Library there.

5 *rien . . . faut*: "nothing develops a young man like an affair with a lady" (French).

6 war: the Crimean War (1853–56) between Russia and an alliance of Britain, France, Sardinia, and the Ottoman Empire.

7 the death of my brother: of Dmitry in 1856, of tuberculosis.

8 peasant schools: in the late 1850s Tolstoy became much concerned with popular education and established a school for the peasants on his estate at Yasnaya Polyana.

9 emancipation of the peasants: this took place in 1861.

10 arbitrator: in the settlement of boundaries or disputes with the peasants.

11 *koumiss*: a drink of fermented mare's milk, often prescribed for health.

12 Samara estate: in 1871, Tolstoy bought a remote estate in Bashkir country where the family could lead the "simple life," drink *koumiss*, etc.

13 Schopenhauer: Arthur Schopenhauer (1788–1860), German philosopher. Tolstoy venerated Schopenhauer for his ideas about the futility of human striving. Schopenhauer was one of the first Western philosophers to seriously study Indian philosophy.

14 Socrates: c. 469–399 B.C., Greek philosopher, one of the founding fathers of Western philosophy.

15 nothing: Tolstoy is quoting from the two last paragraphs of Book IV of Schopenhauer's *The World as Will and Representation* [or *as Idea*], first published in 1819 but later revised. I have used here the first English translation by R. B. Haldane and J. Kemp (London, 1883).

16 sun: from Ecclesiastes, chapters 1, 2, and 9. Tolstoy is quoting from the Synodal Russian Bible of 1876. The translation uses the King James Version with a few very small changes to match the Russian.

17 Shakyamuni: "sage of the Shakyas," an honorific title often given to Gautama Buddha.

18 goest: from Ecclesiastes, chapter 9.

19 Descartes: (1596–1650), French philosopher and mathematician who would have formed part of an "arts" education in Russia, essentially a philosophical one.

20 Kant: (1724–1804), German philosopher of the Enlightenment. His major work is *The Critique of Pure Reason.*

21 resurrection: the Russian name for Sunday—*voskreseniye*—means "resurrection."

22 Tsar's Gates: the central door of the iconostasis in a Russian Orthodox church.

23 Chetyi-Minei and the Prologues: two compilations of the Lives of the Saints.

24 Three years: 1878–1880.

25 catechumen: someone receiving instruction with a view to baptism.

26 Old Believers, Molokans: the former—schismatics who adhered to the liturgical practices from before the reforms of 1652–66; the latter, literally "milk-drinkers"—sectarians who rejected the rituals of the Orthodox Church.

27 Pashkovites: Russian Evangelicals.

28 hermits: in Russian and Eastern Orthodoxy, hermits, singly or in communities, play a significant role.

29 *filioque*: "from the Son", a phrase in the Nicene Creed used by most of the Western churches; together with the primacy of the pope, the main source of schism between Eastern and Western churches.

30 Alexis Mikhailovich: tsar, r. 1645–79, a time of religious reforms.

31 a war: the Russo-Turkish War of 1877–78.

32 young men: he is referring to the execution of revolutionary terrorists.

A NOTE ON THE TRANSLATIONS

by Rosamund Bartlett

A good translator is like a good musician: able to interpret a work in such a way that all one seems to hear is the master's voice. In both cases, there is more than just understanding at stake. Translators and musicians have to perform a fine balancing act, steering on one hand between a strict and accurate rendition of the words or notes on the page and on the other the artistically more truthful conveyance of a meaning relevant to their own particular audience and time. And then comes the even greater challenge of giving an overall shape to one's interpretation, creating a mood and tone that can only come from immersing oneself in the work and listening keenly to its rhythms and cadences. At best, the result is the illusion that translators and musicians are vessels, their own presence unnoticeable. Reading Peter

Carson's new translations of *The Death of Ivan Ilyich* and *Confession*, one certainly has the sensation of coming face-to-face with Lev Nikolayevich Tolstoy in all his rough-and-ready majesty.

Over the course of the twelve years in which I knew Peter as my editor, we both made the transition from Chekhov to Tolstoy as translators, and we used to swap stories about some of the thornier challenges we had tackled as well as the rewards that come from intense study of some of the greatest masterpieces of Russian prose (my position was usually that of the respectful pupil, I hasten to add). It was perhaps unusual to have had an acquiring editor who was also engaged in literary translation, but Peter *was* unusual. When he asked me to edit a collection of Chekhov's letters for Penguin Classics back in 2001 (brilliantly timed to coincide with the appearance of previously censored materials), he already had in his sights new renderings of Chekhov's major plays. His peerless translations, which were published in 2006, effortlessly convey both the grace and the economy of Chekhov's writing and stand out in a crowded market.

In between Chekhov and Tolstoy for Peter came Turgenev, an often unjustly forgotten writer for whom he had a special affinity. Turgenev comes across in his writing as a refined but self-effacing man of exceptional judgment, and I remember Peter in this way too. I initially demurred when approached to write the introduction to his new translation of *Fathers and Sons*, arguing to his editor at Penguin

Classics that I needed to get on with the biography of Tolstoy that Peter had commissioned me to write, but he was politely insistent. He was an editor who helped his authors in numerous unexpected ways, because of course the experience of giving an account of the background of *Fathers and Sons* was the ideal preparation for dealing as a biographer with Turgenev's important but fractious relationship with Tolstoy, which came to a head just after the novel was completed. The bad feeling created by Tolstoy's falling asleep while Turgenev read his new novel to him led to their almost fighting a duel. Tolstoy was immune—well, actually downright hostile—to the delicacy and artistry of Turgenev's writing, but these are qualities to which Peter is exceptionally sensitive in his translation. In order to capture its spirit, he told me he had studied the early French translations, one of which was completed by the author himself in collaboration with his great friend Pauline Viardot in 1863. Since Russian and French were used interchangeably by the nineteenth-century Russian gentry, it was an inspired thing to do. Peter's *Fathers and Sons* is now widely considered to be the most distinguished translation of this great novel in print.

Unlike Tolstoy, the much younger Chekhov was very receptive to the beauty of Turgenev's writing, and the experience of translating their finely chiseled, immaculately crafted prose differs enormously from that of tackling Tolstoy's masterpieces. While Peter was engaged in translating *Confession* and *The Death of Ivan Ilyich*, I was completing a new translation of *Anna Karenina*, and we both found Tolstoy much more difficult. With Turgenev and Chekhov, who seem to stretch a hand out toward the translator, everything appears to have its place, whereas with Tolstoy it often feels more like a battle with an author who does not want to give an inch (a sensation I also had while writing his biography). Well might Vladimir Nabokov describe Tolstoy's style as a "marvelously complicated, ponderous instrument." Here is a writer who, in a defiant assertion of freedom, deliberately rebelled against literary convention, spurning traditional rhetorical devices to create almost a new language in his fictional works. Tolstoy took pride in exhibiting the family trait of wildness (*dikost'*), and it was rather inevitable that this trait showed up in his writing too. Peter Carson shows himself to be more than equal to the task of taming it, however.

Tolstoy was always much more straightforward in his nonfictional writing, and he took care to ensure that *Confession* was particularly lucid, as this was his first attempt to attract a wide audience to his newfound Christian ideas. He came to see himself as living the life of an apostle for the truth with every limb of his body, so he also needed to be persuasive in *Confession*. Even this painfully candid, uncomplicated memoir, however, can give rise to quite differing interpretations in English translation, as can be seen by comparing different versions. Take, for example, the opening sentences of Chapter Four:

Translated by Vladimir Chertkov, 1885:

My life had come to a sudden stop, I was able to breathe, to eat, to drink, to sleep, I could not, indeed, help doing so; but there was no real life in me; I had not a single wish to strive for the fulfillment of what I could feel to be reasonable. . . . Had a fairy appeared and offered me all I desired, I should not have known what to say. . . . I could not even wish to know the truth, because I guessed what the truth was. The truth lay in this, that life had no meaning for me.

Translated by Louise and Aylmer Maude, 1921:

My life came to a standstill. I could breathe, eat, drink, and sleep, and I could not help doing these things; but there was no life, for there were no wishes the fulfillment of which I could consider reasonable. . . . Had a fairy come and offered to fulfill my desires I should not have known what to ask. . . . I could not even wish to know the truth, for I guessed of what it consisted. The truth was that life is meaningless.

Translated by David Patterson, 1983:

My life came to a stop. I could breathe, eat, drink, and sleep; indeed, I could not help but breathe, eat, drink, and sleep. But there was no life in me because I had no desires whose satisfaction I would have found reasonable. . . . If a fairy had come and offered to fulfill my every wish, I would not have known what to wish for. . . . I did not even want to discover truth anymore because I had guessed what it was. The truth was that life is meaningless.

Translated by Jane Kentish, 1987:

My life came to a standstill. I could breathe, eat, drink and sleep and I could not help breathing, eating, drinking and sleeping; but there was no life in me because I had no desires whose gratification I would have deemed it reasonable to fulfill. . . . If a magician had come and offered to grant my wishes I would not have known what to say. . . . I did not even wish to know the truth because I had guessed what it was. The truth was that life is meaningless.

Translated by Peter Carson, 2013:

My life came to a halt. I could breathe, eat, drink, sleep, and I couldn't *not* breathe, eat, drink, sleep; but I had no life because I had no desires in the fulfillment of which I might find any meaning. . . . If an enchantress had come and offered to fulfill my desires for me, I wouldn't have known what to say. . . . I could not even desire to learn the truth because I guessed wherein it lay. The truth was that life is nonsense.

What is particularly successfully rendered in English here by Peter Carson is the abruptness of the first sentence (*moya zhizn' ostanovilas'*—literally, "my life stopped"); the felicitous translation of *volshebnitsa* as "enchantress" (the gender is definitely female; "fairy" sounds all wrong); the boldly colloquial "couldn't," emulating Tolstoy's preference for the living, spoken language; and the use of "nonsense," accurately reflecting the nuances of the Russian (Tolstoy writes *zhizn' est' bessmyslitsa*, rather than *zhizn' bessmyslenna*).

In the fiction that Tolstoy wrote after *Anna Karenina*, he consciously tried to simplify his famously convoluted writing style. In this he was partially successful. *The Death of Ivan Ilyich*, certainly, is devoid of some of the extremes to be found in *Anna Karenina*—ninety-eight word sentences, clusters of as many as five adjectives in a row, and multiple subordinate clauses packed with participles and gerunds like sardines in a tin. Consummate artist to the last that he was, however, Tolstoy could not refrain from deploying sophisticated narrative strategies in his methods of constructing *The Death of Ivan Ilyich*, which range from stream of consciousness to the manipulation of Christian imagery for his own ends. In Peter Carson, Tolstoy has a translator alert to all of his carefully concealed complexities and the idiosyncrasies of his style, but above all to the simplicity on the surface of his writing.

Most characteristic of Tolstoy's style throughout his literary career is his use of repetition. Peter's translation faithfully preserves the dozens of instances where we encounter variations of the word "pleasant" (*priyatno*), for example (there are sixteen in Chapter Two alone), which are fundamental to elaborating on the theme of reversal in the story and communicating its overall ironic tone. Peter also proves wonderfully inventive when relaying Tolstoy's sardonic sense of humor. Take, for example, the famous scene in Chapter One in which Pyotr Ivanovich visits Ivan Ilyich's grieving widow. The lugubrious solemnity of the occasion is immediately punctured when he has to do battle with a rebellious pouf (*buntovavshiisya pod nim puf*), and Tolstoy thus forces the reader to see through the veneer of hypocrisy. The passage has been rendered in many different ways, and we might compare two more recent translations of how it begins with Peter's neat version:

Translated by Anne Pasternak-Slater, 2003:

> They entered her dimly lit sitting room, upholstered in pink cretonne, and sat down by a table—she on a divan, Piotr Ivanovich on a low ottoman, whose broken springs yielded unpredictably to his weight.

Translated by Richard Pevear and Larissa Volokhonsky, 2009:

> Having gone into her drawing room, upholstered in pink cretonne and with a sullen lamp, they sat by the table, she on the sofa, Pyotr Ivanovich on a low pouf with bad springs that gave way erratically under his weight.

Translated by Peter Carson, 2013:

> They went into her dimly lit drawing room hung with pink cretonne and sat down by a table, she on a sofa and Pyotr Ivanovich on a low pouf built on springs that awkwardly gave way as he sat down.

Peter Carson is scrupulous and attentive throughout *The Death of Ivan Ilyich*, producing an English version that respects Tolstoy and all his rough edges, yet is always a pleasure to read. His Tolstoy translations are sure to stand the test of time.

ACKNOWLEDGMENTS

I am grateful for the support and encouragement of my editor Robert Weil and his team at W. W. Norton. Also to my wife Eleo and daughter Charlotte.

—*Peter Carson*

Peter was not well enough to write his own introduction. However, he would have been thrilled and honored that two authors to whom he was close stepped in at the final stages: Mary Beard, who wrote the introduction, and Rosamund Bartlett, who wrote A Note on the Translations.

—*Eleo Carson*

ABOUT THE TRANSLATOR

PETER CARSON studied Russian while on national service in the British Navy at the Joint Services School for Linguists in Scotland and London. At home he spoke Russian—his mother Tatiana Staheyeff and her family escaped from Russia during the Bolshevik Revolution. His working life was spent on the editorial side of publishing where for many years he was editor in chief of Penguin Books in the UK. In 1998 he was asked by Andrew Franklin to join him at Profile Books and he worked with his authors until his death in January 2013.

A professor of classics at Cambridge University, MARY BEARD is the author of the best-selling *The Fires of Vesuvius.* A popular blogger and television presenter, she contributes frequently to the *New York Review of Books.* She lives in England.

ROSAMUND BARTLETT is a scholar, writer, and translator whose books include acclaimed biographies of Chekhov and Tolstoy, as well as edited volumes on Shostakovich and the Futurist opera *Victory over the Sun*. Her Chekhov anthology *About Love and Other Stories* was shortlisted for the Weidenfeld Translation Prize, while her *Chekhov: A Life in Letters* is the first uncensored edition in any language. Her new translation of *Anna Karenina* will be published by Oxford World's Classics in 2014.